Title: Coming Up Cuban

Author: Sonia Manzano

On-Sale Date: August 2, 2022

Format: Jacketed Hardcover

ISBN: 978-1-338-06515-2 ‖ Price: $18.99 US

Ages: 8–12

Grades: 3–7

LOC Number: Available

Length: 320 pages

Trim: 5-1/2 x 8-1/4 inches

Classification: Young Adult novel on Cuban revolution

---------------- *Additional Formats Available* --------------

Ebook ISBN: 978-1-338-06532-9

Digital Audiobook ISBN: 978-1-338-80127-9 ‖ Price: $20.99

Library Audiobook ISBN: 978-1-338-80128-6 ‖ Price: $62.99

Scholastic Press
An Imprint of Scholastic Inc.
557 Broadway, New York, NY 10012
For information, contact us at:
tradepublicity@scholastic.com

D0190455

Dear Reader,

My parents used an expression, *Buscarse la vida*, to describe why they migrated to the mainland from Puerto Rico in the late 1940s. *Buscarse la vida* means "to find one's life." In this novel, I present four separate stories of young Cubans who have to find their lives after Fidel Castro's revolution in 1959.

I was reminded of my parents' Puerto Rican expression while crafting the narratives and voices of the young people whose plights and triumphs drive these stories. While researching, I read how quickly their situations were changed by Castro's revolution. Suddenly, Cuban social classes had to redefine themselves and find other ways to live. Of course, I was most interested in the effects all this had on the young. How did changes affect twelve- and thirteen-year-olds thrown into new circumstances?

Immersing myself in this topic, I read about revolutionary zeal gone wrong, unaccompanied minors sent to the USA, and political initiatives meted out to those left behind. I imagined how those changes might have affected young Cubans on the cusp of making sense of and forming opinions about the world around them.

Then I got to work telling those tales through the fictitious lives of Ana, Miguel, Zulema, and Juan. Ana is the disenchanted daughter of a revolutionary. Miguel, part of Operation Pedro Pan, a slightly clandestine exodus of unaccompanied minors, is sent away to the USA by parents who feared for his safety. Zulema is an illiterate *guajira* peasant girl struggling with dormant yearnings of her own, and Juan, a poor Afro Cubano living in a Havana slum, struggles with feelings of loyalty. Unbeknownst to them, but clear to us, their lives brush up against one another's.

Right now, the world is full of contradictions. Subtle disparities in attitudes are exposed as deep divides. Young people everywhere will need to have faith in themselves to *buscarse la vida*—find their lives.

My faith in myself made me navigate through adolescent minefields to find my way clear to audition for, and create, the character Maria on *Sesame Street*. The faith my characters Ana, Miguel, Zulema, and Juan have in themselves makes them prevail because, as usual, the young will see their way out of darkness. Someday the rest of us will follow suit. This is what I hope to suggest to readers of *Coming Up Cuban*.

Sonia Manzano

Sonia Manzano

PRAISE FOR SONIA MANZANO'S
The Revolution of Evelyn Serrano

A Pura Belpré Honor Book
Winner of the Américas Award

★ "[S]tunning." —*Kirkus Reviews*, starred review

★ "[W]ry, moving." —*Booklist*, starred review

"Sonia Manzano vividly portrays a neighborhood in turmoil,
with embraceable characters who change history."
—Pam Muñoz Ryan, Newbery Honor–winning author of *Echo*

"Should be placed on proud display with the literature
that enriches our multicultural America."
—Julia Alvarez, Pura Belpré Award–winning author of
Before We Were Free and *How the García Girls Lost Their Accents*

"This novel is meant to be savored."
—Oscar Hijuelos, Pulitzer Prize–winning author of
The Mambo Kings Play Songs of Love

"Thank you, Sonia Manzano . . . for reminding us that history
doesn't just happen. We live with it, and its consequences."
—Esmeralda Santiago, Alex Award–winning author of
Almost a Woman and *When I Was Puerto Rican*

Praise for *Becoming Maria:*
Love and Chaos in the South Bronx

"Manzano is such a familiar figure in our pop culture that it would be almost easy to miss that she is an ink-slinging story-teller with serious smarts and unquestionable literary gifts."
—Veronica Chambers, *The New York Times*

★ "[A] poignantly written memoir."
—*School Library Journal*, starred review

★ "Manzano paints a poignant, startlingly honest picture of her youth."
—*Kirkus Reviews*, starred review

"[A] voice that conveys a slow-burning audacity and the internal glimmer of lightness of a true dreamer."
—*Publishers Weekly*

COMING UP
CUBAN

COMING UP CUBAN

SONIA MANZANO

SCHOLASTIC PRESS

New York

Library of Congress Cataloging-in-Publication Data available
ISBN 978-1-338-06515-2

10 9 8 7 6 5 4 3 2 1   22 23 24 25 26

Printed in the U.S.A.   128
First edition, August 2022

Book design by Abby Dening and Elizabeth B. Parisi

To my bighearted daughter, Gabriela Rose Reagan, who always sees the other person's point of view

Torn Together

1959 · 1960 · 1961

*When your tears of hope and betrayal turn shooting stars
soft and out of focus . . .*

When you discover who you are in a foreign country . . .

When learning to read makes you hate your father . . .

*When a red bubble of blood from a pinprick on your
finger signals pain and violence you can't outrun . . .*

*That is when you are rising past Fidel Castro's shadow
and* Coming Up Cuban.

Ana, Miguel, Zulema, and Juan are each aching to escape the ugly ways of a rebel leader whose suffocating rules and ideas compel them to fight for their lives and blood relationships. Ultimately, they are forced to cling to what they believe is right— even as government rules threaten to quiet their voices.

As bombings and betrayals tear their lives and families apart, Ana, Miguel, Zulema, and Juan stand together, their hearts brimming with hope as they share the common dream of controlling their own destinies.

*The dagger plunged in the name of freedom
is plunged into the breast of freedom.*

—JOSÉ MARTÍ, CUBAN POET

ANA

HAVANA, CUBA · 1959

We are almost there. Almost at the gate. Chispa, my dog, afraid of the gunshots sounding sharp in the distance, is whimpering in my arms. My mother is just ahead—so close, so close to home—when the rebel grabs her!

She squeals! Fear weakens and drains me—but the blood pumping through my body propels me forward. I run and jump onto the rebel's back—my skirt rides up as my legs hook around his waist. His filthy shirt, belt, pants feel slick and grimy against my thighs, but I hang on tight, squeezing with my knees and punching with my fists. He grunts and twists in surprise as Mami gulps air like a stupid seal.

Chispa, who had been so afraid of the celebratory gunshots, is now brave, and my little dog, even while dropped and lost in the tangles of her leash and our bodies, finds a way to latch onto the man's ankle.

"*Caramba,*" the man curses.

"Stop," Mami pleads.

But the man won't stop. So, like Chispa, I bite. Right into his ear!

"*Ahggg . . .*" he grunts, twisting, trying to flick us both away.

The top rubbery part of his ear is disgustingly salty. Hair from his head that slips into my mouth tastes like pennies.

"Stop, Ana, I told you to stop!" screams my mother, pulling at me.

Me? Did I hear right? Was she talking to me? I find her face over his dirty shoulder. The look in her eyes is wild, crazy, and . . . happy? "Ana, Ana," she says forcefully. "Stop! I said stop!"

The man's sour breath hits my face.

She says it again. "Stop!"

The man makes another sound and, grabbing his ear, maneuvers away from me. "*¡Caramba!*" But this time he chuckles.

Chispa's barking joins the sounds of cracks in the sky. My mother, calmer now, whispers hoarsely, "Stop! I said stop! It's your father, Ana! It's your father!"

Papi

I try to calm my heart long enough to look in his face, past the hair that covers it. And slowly, like muddy water settling and becoming clear, his face comes into focus and I see it *is* my father. I shake my head to understand, to take it all in, but I can't.

"Ana, it's me. I am sorry to have scared you," he says in a voice that is rough and unrecognizable. "*Caramba*, my ear . . ."

My father? Who had been gone so long? Who had joined the rebel fighters in the Sierra Maestra mountains? Who left us to fight in the Revolution?

I feel small, crazy, embarrassed as we stumble and roll, through the gate, into the house.

Inside, stunned, I watch and listen as my mother and father chatter and kiss and try to pull me toward them. But I pull back. He stinks.

"We did it! We won, Lydia. Fidel and our rebels have won," he says. "Corrupt dictator Batista is out!"

"I missed you so," Mami murmurs. "Ana, come . . ."

But it's too much.

"Don't worry, Lydia," he says, laughing, holding on to his ear. "Ana has not seen me in almost two years. She probably doesn't recognize me." He stares at me. "I hardly recognize her. You look taller than the girl I left behind, Ana. Quite a bite you have there too." He examines my face as though I am a photo. "Same freckles though, same light brown eyes." Chispa growls. "And who is this?"

"Chispa! We got her while you were gone," says Mami.

The man reaches to pet Chispa. "Trying to take my place, huh, doggie?"

Chispa growls.

"You are so skinny!" says Mami.

"I need a bath!" he answers, smiling at me reluctantly. "And a bandage for my ear."

My parents swirl upstairs, leaving me alone in the room, spinning like a top, panting like Chispa. Through the noise of the shower, I think I hear my mother say, "¡Batista se fue! ¡Llegó Fidel!"

My father repeats her words. "Batista is out! Fidel had arrived!"

His words ring in my ear.

Victory

"Do you see him, Ana? Do you see your father?"

How can I recognize my father? All these rebels look alike! Long hair and beards.

"Do you see him?" she repeats.

We are at a victory parade looking for Papi, but all I see are crazy-looking hairy men in trucks and jeeps. The crowd all along the Malecón roadway presses me forward, screaming, *"¡Viva Cuba libre!"* I hear my own grandmother, aunts, and uncles yelling the loudest. They pop up and down, peeking through the crowd to get a better look at them. My family reminds me of cartoon characters in a show from the United States.

"¡Viva Cuba libre!" the crowd roars again and again.

"Do you see him?" my mother asks me again, like a broken record. She is the only one not screaming, but breathless like an American movie star in a love story. "Do you see him?"

The heat makes me weak, and I feel about to faint when all at once the screams get as sharp as sirens. *"¡Fidel! ¡Fidel!"* The cries jerk me up.

On a platform, on the back of a flatbed truck, is the revolutionary leader himself—Fidel Castro!

He waves. All hands, black, brown, and white, reach out as one. He waves again and again as everyone cheers madly. He seems taller than anyone I have ever seen and makes me think of a stallion with wings. His hair is thick and black and flies off his wide forehead like the waves of the Caribbean Sea behind us. His face is divided by a long nose that looks about to snort. He holds his cigar in his mouth like a weapon that can shoot or explode any second.

"There he is!" My mother's lips move again. But she is not pointing at Fidel. She is pointing to my father in the jeep behind Fidel.

My father spots us, and stares so hard I feel pinned against something.

His jeep passes us.

Mami bends down and screams in my ear, "Did you see how close he was to Fidel Castro? Just one vehicle behind! Did you see?"

I nod yes as my eardrum vibrates from her voice. She turns me around and shoves a red-and-black revolutionary flag into my hand.

"Did you see how close your father was to Fidel? That is because your father is very, very important to the Revolution! He helped Fidel win! Wave your flag, Ana. Wave your flag!"

I do what she says.

Papi Snacks

I call my best friend, Carmen. "Yes—he's back. In the living room having chunks of skin ripped off him." Carmen laughs. "No—I'm kidding," I go on. "But that's what my grandmother keeps doing! She keeps hugging and kissing him and grabbing at him so hard I think she'd like to break a chunk off him, just to make sure he is for real. Ha! But who am I to say? I almost bit his ear off."

"Ana! Come for a *croqueta!*" calls out my mother.

"What did his *ear* taste like?" teases Carmen. "Like chicken . . . ?"

"Ha! I'll tell you when I see you. Mami's calling me." Then Carmen asks me if I think our teacher, Sister Michelle, wears a bra!

"Ana . . ." Mami calls out.

"No, Carmen, I don't think Sister Michelle wears a bra! I think she wears a sling because it looks like she only has one big, round breast that goes down to her waist!" With that, I hang up, giggling, and sneak into the living room.

My father and I accidentally lock eyes for a moment. We never look at each other at the same time. I look and he turns away—or he looks and I turn away. Maybe he is mad because I bit him.

Getting my pad and pencil, I lose myself in drawing the lines and shape and shadows of the ear I almost ate.

"Tell us about fighting in the mountains!" my family pleads as my mother runs to the kitchen to get him more food he can't eat because he *just* ate.

"I'd rather tell you about how Ana almost bit my ear off!"

I'm so surprised he mentioned me I think there is some *other* Ana in the room he's talking about. But I am saved from responding by a knock on the door. My father answers.

"Antonio," my father calls out, letting in a man with a face full of so many pimples I decide to give him a new name— Pimple-Face! "*¿Qué tal?*" says my father, forgetting all about me. "This is my *compañero* Antonio," he announces to everyone. "We fought together!"

Pimple-Face pats my father's back, saying, "And this man, this man, Rafael Andino, saved my life."

My family gasps.

"And now Antonio and I will help form this new government!" adds my father, throwing his arm around his buddy-boy-pal.

I've got to call Carmen and tell her about this man with a mountain range of pimples, but nobody picks up. Nobody home. They probably went for ice cream. I wish we could go for ice cream. Instead I am forced to listen to the conversation going on in the living room. The Revolution this, and the Revolution that . . . I thought the Revolution was over.

But actually, it was just beginning.

Not Knowing You

I am outside counting the bullet holes in my father's jeep when my mother calls out from the house, "Ana, why don't you and Papi find the fruit seller! I need some oranges!"

My father steps out and we quickly look away from each other as we get into the jeep. I had counted eighteen bullet holes but say nothing as we drive around silently. Finally, we hear the old Black fruit seller singing, *¡Frutas, naranjas dulces!* We park, then approach the cart. The seller's helper, a boy about my age, slowly takes in the bullet holes, my father, and me. I peek at the boy's long dark legs as my father picks out the oranges and starts to pay for them—but the old man stops him.

"No, *señor*. For you, free!" He smiles, but his eyes are wary and cautious—curious about the bullet holes.

"No, I will pay for it," says my father, pressing money into the old man's trembling hand. "No reason for you to give it to me for free. And you don't have to call me *señor*. We are comrades now."

The fruit seller does not agree or disagree. He simply takes the money, coughs softly, spits, and signals the boy to move on. *¡Frutas, naranjas dulces!* he sings uncertainly.

We get into the jeep.

"See that fruit seller and that boy?" My father sighs.

"What?"

"That fruit seller and his helper."

"Of course." Did my father think I was blind?

"What do you see?"

I don't know what he's talking about, but I look. All I see is an old man with knotted white hair sticking out from under an old straw hat, and his helper. There are lots of fruit sellers like that in Havana.

But my father insists. "Look at them! Ana, open your eyes."

I look at them again.

"What? It's just the fruit seller," I say.

"Look harder. What do you see?"

"I see an old man who spits a lot and a boy in an undershirt with long legs, scabby knees, and big feet forced into sandals . . ."

"But who *is* he?" my father presses.

"I don't know—the old man's grandson?" I feel like I am taking a test.

"Yes, probably—but don't you think he is someone who deserves proper shoes and clothes?" My father goes on, "Think about his life—that boy is about your age—do you think he goes to school?"

"I don't know . . ." I say. I had never thought of boys like that going to school.

"He probably hangs out at the dump—I used to see kids like him, looking for things in the dump to sell, all the time. And I bet that that old man, yes, probably his *abuelo*, has never seen a doctor. Did you notice that cough?"

I noticed his spitting too, ugh—but say nothing.

ANA

"This Revolution was fought to end a dictatorship. A dictatorship that made us unequal." His voice lifts with excitement.

Then he says, "What do you think, Ana?"

"About what?"

"Everything," he says, smiling.

I think I see a path opening between us, but I'm not sure what to say so I grab at anything. "I'm sorry I bit you."

He laughs. "It's all right, my ear still works. See?"

And then he wiggles it!

Portrait

The portraits I've drawn are scattered all over.

"These are my friends Carmen and Norma . . ." I say, treading softly.

"What are they like?" he asks.

"Well, Carmen is skinny and wears her black hair in curls all around her head . . . and never wants to do what her mother wants her to do."

"So, she's a rebel?" he says, grinning.

"I guess so . . . I had never thought of her like that. But yes."

"And is this Norma? Is she sad?"

"No, she just looks that way because her eyes and shoulders droop."

He laughs before going on. "So you have a rebel friend and a droopy friend—and you are the artist friend. You are a great *artista*."

Suddenly I can't show him my drawings fast enough.

"That's my mother," he says, massaging his arm.

"Yes," I say, giggling.

"And that's Chispa!"

"Yes."

"She doesn't like me."

"No . . ."

Then he says, "Why don't you draw me? I'll sit perfectly still," he offers. "Draw my profile." Then he turns the other way. "No, this way . . . so you can draw the ear I almost lost!"

My face reddens.

"You did the right thing," he adds. "You were brave."

"Like you were brave fighting in the Sierra Maestra?"

"I wasn't always brave. Sometimes I was so afraid I cried, and wanted the fighting to stop."

"So why didn't you stop the fighting and come home?" I ask carefully.

"Because I was too busy hoping we would win. And we did!"

My mother enters with a tray of fritters. "Did somebody say *hope*? I have hope too. I hope you eat these," she commands.

My father and I roll our eyes.

"What's going on?" says my mother, confused.

This time my father and I look straight at each other and smile.

Photograph

"Eighteen!" says Carmen, tapping around the bullet hole with her pink nail. I count eighteen bullet holes.

"No wonder bullets kill people," says Norma. "Look what they did to this jeep!"

My father joins us.

"That's right—and they wanted to shoot my father eighteen times!" I say quickly. "That proves he was a really *special* rebel."

"Now, now," Papi scolds warmly. "Revolution is not a game."

"I know, but still . . ."

My mother comes down the steps wearing a dress with orange flowers and red flowers. They look so real I think they might attract butterflies. On the way to our picnic, we pass rebel soldiers coming from the opposite direction. My father reaches under his seat and pulls out a carton of cigarettes. "Lydia—toss them to the soldiers," he says.

"Can *I* do it? They look so cute!" says Norma wistfully, fingering the heart-shaped pendant on her necklace as if she wants the soldiers to see it.

"I'll do it," says Mami. As she tosses the individual packs to the soldiers, her gorgeous dress flaps like flowers in the breeze, making soldiers cheer and roar and wave.

"Papi looked just like them when he got home, only much dirtier and much more disgusting. He smelled too."

My mother and father laugh from the front seat. Papi wiggles his ears, making Norma giggle.

At the picnic, Mami gives my father the biggest servings of food, saying, "I have to fatten you up!"

"Lydia, I met people skinnier than me when I was fighting in the mountains," he grins. "I met farmers, *guajiros*, who were so skinny, they had to tighten their belts every morning. Who were so poor, they lived without electricity or running water. Whose hands were so ruined by work, they could hardly make a fist."

"Wait! What? They couldn't make a fist?" I say.

"No, they couldn't. Their hands were so swollen they could hardly hold a spoon or a pencil."

I grab my pencil, imagining what it would be like if I couldn't hold it straight.

My father goes on, "Those people can't read or write, but were so proud they swept their dirt floors every day."

"Dirt floors? They had dirt floors?" says Carmen, amazed.

Suddenly his voice becomes charged. "It's not fair that people live like that."

"No . . . I guess it's not fair," whispers Carmen.

My father lowers his voice as well. "Still—these *guajiros* shared whatever food there was with us rebels—even bits of coconut meat."

"Coconut meat?" says Carmen, amazed.

My father puts images in my head that I must get down on

paper. When he looks off, I try to see what he sees so hard, I bite my lip.

Carmen suddenly announces, "I'm going to help those people with swollen hands and dirt floors, somehow, when I grow up. Maybe even be a teacher—and never get married, like my mother wants me to," she adds.

"Good! I am going to marry one of those cute soldiers who just passed us and live happily ever after! *If* he can wiggle his ears," adds Norma, touching the pendant on her necklace to her lips.

"Ugh," says Carmen, but she laughs right along.

Mami pulls out her camera. "Let's take a picture."

The three of us crowd together on the blanket. "Smile!" she says. Then, "Oh, come on, you girls can do better than that!"

"I'll get them to smile," says my father. He stands behind her and wiggles his ears, making us giggle. As Mami snaps away, a sudden breeze makes the skirt of her dress lick back, through and around my father's legs. Time stops when suddenly, to me, they look like a couple forever blended and wrapped in orange flowers and red flowers.

As she takes a picture of us with her Brownie camera, I take a better picture of them with my mind.

Show, Tell

Finally! The time has come for me to show my drawings in school. I am so excited it feels as if they are burning a hole right through my book bag. "These are drawings of my father and his time in the Revolution!" I announce as I slide them into the projector. Carmen and Norma clap!

"Here is a drawing of a *guajiro*'s hand so swollen with work they cannot make a fist," I say. "They are very poor and cannot read or write."

"People who can't read? They must be very stupid."

I look up. It's Lizzette. She is examining a strand of her long ginger-colored hair. The tiny gold hoops on her ears glisten.

"Quiet," says Sister Michelle sharply. Then she adds, crossing herself along her one breast, "We must always pray for those who have less than we have. Let's move on."

"Some *guajiros* are so poor they live in houses with dirt floors they sweep every day!" I say, showing my next drawing.

"How do they know when a dirt floor is clean?" It's Lizzette again.

My face goes red with anger as I go to the next one. "Here's my father eating coconuts with his comrades and *guajiros* when there was nothing else to eat!"

"They must've gotten diarrhea," interrupts Lizzette once again, carefully splitting the hair as far as it will go.

This time everybody laughs.

Sister Michelle One-Breast glares at us. "That's all the time we have for today, class."

I grab my drawings and seethe until the end of the day.

"Don't be upset, Ana," says Carmen. "Lizzette made fun of your drawing because she's rich."

"I thought it was because she was stupid," adds Norma, playing with her necklace. We laugh.

"It's not funny," says Carmen suddenly.

But Norma and I are still laughing when Lizzette's fancy white car pulls up, followed by my father in the jeep.

"What's so funny?" he asks the minute I climb in.

"See that girl pulling away in the white car—that's Lizzette; she's rich and she made fun of my drawings. She thinks the Revolution is stupid. We're laughing at how stupid *she* is!"

"Ahhh . . ." he says. "Maybe not stupid. Maybe she's just afraid of change. Listen to me, Ana. Changes can excite or frighten people."

"I'm not scared," I say quickly. "I mean—I try not to be afraid."

"That's the best we can do," he says.

Then I ask, "Did you get diarrhea after eating the coconuts?"

He throws his head back, laughing. "Yes—but don't draw a picture of that!"

Scary Movies

"Enjoy the movie," says my father, dropping us off near the movie theater. "Which movie are you going to see?"

"Who cares," says Carmen.

"We love all the movies from the United States! Especially the love stories," adds Norma.

"I'll pick you up in a few hours!" he says, driving away.

Carmen, Norma, and I run to the theater but then stop in our tracks. The movie theater is closed! "Wait—huh? How long has it been closed?" I ask nobody.

"I don't know," says Carmen. "I wonder what happened."

We stare as if staring will make the movie house reopen. I look back for my father, but he is gone.

"Let's buy candy and then just walk around," suggests Norma.

We race to a candy shop and are just about to buy some waxy orange sweets when a man screaming, "Help me! Help me!" almost crashes into the store!

The store owner pushes him out, saying, "No, not here! Get out! I cannot help you! ¡Fuera de aquí!"

The man's eyes bug out looking right at me before turning away. The store owner tries to shove us under the counter, but not before we see a policeman run by, yelling, "Stop!"

Rushing out, we see the man collapse in a heap just down the street. The people around stand aside and watch as the policeman cracks the man on his head, even as he lies there.

"That policeman didn't have to hit him," I say, sucking in my breath.

"He must've done something wrong," says Carmen.

"I want to go home," says Norma.

A police car drives up. People watch as they drag the man away, then go back to strolling around as if nothing had happened.

"They didn't have to crack him on the head when he was down!" I say again.

"Maybe he was against the Revolution!" says Carmen.

"I want to go home," Norma repeats.

We hear drumming and chanting in the distance.

"Let's go see what's over there," I say, trying to change the subject. Following the Canadian tourists gawking, we get to a gathering of Black people practicing *santería*. The women dance, wearing big colorful skirts and head wraps, and wave fragrant small shrubs around their heads. The men are dressed in white and suck on cigars, making huge puffy clouds of smoke.

"You think it's okay for us to get close?" asks Norma.

"Why not?" I say.

"Fidel says practicing religion is bad for Cuba," says Carmen.

"What about our religion? We go to Catholic school remember?" I snap.

"Why are you yelling at me?" says Carmen.

ANA

But policemen come before I can answer, and the *santeros'* shrubs are no match for the policemen's waving sticks, which land hard on people's arms and legs. Carmen, Norma, and I pull one another away and run.

"Why are the police stopping them from dancing?" I cry out.

"I don't know . . . it's different now," insists Carmen.

"What do you mean?" I demand. "How is it different?"

"I don't know," she replies angrily.

"I just want to go home," says Norma, pulling at her necklace.

We find ourselves in front of the movie theater, panting and raging. Norma continues to pull at her necklace. Carmen looks into the distance. For the first time, we can't think of anything to say to one another.

News

"Mami, look!" I call out, gasping.

My mother comes into the room. "What's wrong?"

I point to images of bloodied people on television. "What is that? What's going on?"

My mother's eyes are wide, shocked, before she answers, "Turn it off!"

But I don't want to turn it off. I want to see the news footage of the woman with the white dress and bloodied head. I want to see the man I know is dead because he lies on the ground with a newspaper over his face. I want to see the wall covered with the blood of the people executed against it . . . but Mami snaps the television off.

"What is the meaning of all this violence?" Mami demands to know the minute my father walks in the door.

"Calm down, Lydia. Calm down," says Papi. "These are isolated cases. Some overenthusiastic rebels, maybe, acting on their own. I don't know. Try to calm down. Put it out of your mind."

My mother purses her lips and goes into the kitchen and bangs the pots and pans around as she makes dinner. Papi pats my knee. "Don't worry, *hija*."

"But why is this happening, Papi?"

He takes a breath and holds it in. "I don't know," he says, letting the breath out.

My face feels like a fist.

"Trust me, things will turn out all right. Put this out of your mind," he says.

But I can't put the television images out of my mind. The woman in the bloodied white dress, the dead man with the newspaper covering his face, or the bloodied wall people are shot against. I can't keep the image of the man being cracked on the head or the people being hit for practicing *santería* out of my mind either.

My father pushes a smile through his face. "Think of the new government as a seesaw trying to balance itself," he says. "It's going to go to both extremes before it rights itself. Don't worry, these . . . events . . . will end soon."

But they don't end. We see them on television and in the newspapers, like sparks that come up, die down, then burn bright again. Day in and day out. Until it seems like normal.

Like a new normal.

It's awful what you can get used to.

Explosion

Frutas, naranjas dulces . . . sings the fruit seller in the Parque Central Plaza. My father and I are going for ice cream when— *boom!* There is an explosion! The plaza fills with acrid smoke, and paper flyers float down like a blanket of feathers from above.

Papi shoves my head under his arm and pulls me down on the ground, where I see sandaled, shoed, and high-heeled feet scurrying, twisting, and turning all around. The fruit seller and his grandson have more to deal with—the fruit cart, the oranges, and the old man's cough.

The police come. They push us all back, away from the truck, and examine the area. "It was the ice-cream truck that exploded!" they announce importantly, as if we didn't know, as if we hadn't been right there. They talk, pointing to the building where the flyers are coming from even as they try to gather them before anyone can read them. But I manage to grab one— my father takes it from me, reads it, folds it, and puts it in his pocket. "This is the work of counterrevolutionaries," he whispers. "People against Fidel! This is bad."

Out of the corner of my eye I see the old fruit seller stumble and cough into the crook of his elbow—the smoke is too much for him. The grandson holds the old man up with one hand as if he were a baby, while trying to balance the cart with the other. But when the old man tries to help, it's a mess that unfolds in slow motion. The old man falls. The boy drops everything to catch and cradle him, and then they sadly watch their cart crash into a bench, with the oranges rolling everywhere.

Fear and anger that had been hiding in the corners of my mind explode out into the open.

"Can you just tell Fidel that he should do something to make it stop? That trucks shouldn't explode in the park when people are trying to buy ice cream or sell oranges."

"What? ¿Qué?" My father looks stunned, confused.

"Papi, you heard me!"

"Calm down."

"I can't calm down, Papi—why should men get cracked on the head even when they are down? And why shouldn't people practice santería if they want to, like they always did, without getting pushed around?" And then I bury my face into my father's waist, but he sees my tears anyway.

His eyes get soft and round with worry and sorrow, with deeper lines and shadows than I could ever draw.

"Papi, what happened to that woman in the bloody white dress we saw on television? Or that man lying on the street with the newspaper over his face? Why are people being executed against walls? Was it supposed to be like this? Is this what you thought would happen after the Revolution?"

His eyes go from round worry to straight determination. "Let's go!" he says.

Back home, Papi paces the room, telling Mami that he will

knock some sense into his comrades! She makes *café* as I sharpen his pencils and he writes draft after draft of his thoughts to send to the newspapers.

Mami asks him if speaking out is safe.

"Why wouldn't it be safe?" I ask before he can answer. "Why wouldn't it be safe?"

"Of course it's safe," he assures me. "This is not a dictatorship. Just writing my opinion to send to newspapers will not get me killed in this new Cuba!"

He manages a smile, but I feel a storm coming.

Papi's Arrest

Days later, a window's shutter bangs, announcing the storm's arrival.

"Close that shutter!" Mami shouts out from the kitchen.

But it's not the shutter making noise. It's someone banging on the door. Chispa's hackles rise. When Papi goes to see, two policemen barge in with the weather. One of them is his buddy-boy-pal, Antonio, Pimple-Face!

"Rafael Andino, you are under arrest!" Antonio says, pointing to my father.

"Antonio? Is this some kind of joke?" says my father.

"I am afraid not, Rafael. This is no joke," says Antonio. "You are under arrest!"

The other policeman watches closely.

"Antonio, you're talking to *me*! Your *compañero*. We fought together . . ."

"I know, Rafael." Then Pimple-Face tries to pull him aside, whispering urgently, "We did fight together. We fought for the Revolution. We fought for Fidel—but you've changed. You keep writing these articles. People are calling you an anti-Fidel."

"But that's ridiculous. I'm not against Fidel," says my father. "I just want to point out some problems. That's all!"

Antonio leans in close and warns hoarsely, "But sending these articles to the newspapers? Are you crazy?" he says. "Let's go."

"No! Wait! Don't take him," I cry out. How can I lose my father again when I feel as though I just met him!

Papi bends down, holding me close. Mami scoops down and wraps her arms around both of us. "Rafael . . ."

"We don't want you to go," I cry.

"I have a job for you," he says to me, suddenly standing tall. "I want you to help your mother." She falls against him, even as he helps her up.

"But—but, you said . . ." I fumble around, quickly trying to remember his words. "You said, this Revolution was about ending a dictatorship . . ."

"Now it's about helping your mother and the family until I get back!" he says sharply. Then he whispers something in Mami's ear.

She looks at him, panicked. "No . . ." she answers. "I couldn't!"

"You must," he says. He turns to me as Antonio shoves him out the door. "I hope I can count on you, Ana!" Then Papi wiggles his ears at me! How can he wiggle his ears at me at a time like this! Did he think I was the same kid he left behind when he went to fight in the Revolution? I wasn't. My mother sags against the door. I grab the phone and dial my grandmother. "Here," I say, offering her the mouthpiece. "Talk to Grandmother. Tell her! You must!"

She blinks, takes the phone, and pulls on her hair nervously as I listen to one side of the conversation. I can hear my grandmother's scream at the other end of the line. "The family will come tomorrow," says Mami, finally hanging up. Then she makes coffee she forgets to drink.

"Your father will be back before we know it," she says.

Mami's shoulders cave in as she goes into her room. Her soft sobs are the only things holding her up. Chispa and I follow her as the sobs give way and she collapses onto her bed. I take off her shoes and pull the thin blanket around her. Then I go back into the kitchen and drink the cold coffee, feeling much older than I did yesterday.

Secrets

I carry the weight of Papi's arrest in my heart, but I have to tell someone.

"Huh?" Carmen gasps. "But your father was a rebel! How could he have been arrested by rebels? How can that be?"

"Yes, how can that be?" says Norma.

But Sister Michelle One-Breast interrupts us with more shocking news.

"Lizzette will not be coming back to school," she says. "Her family is moving to Miami."

"Fidel took over her father's perfume factory. I saw it announced on television! So her family left as soon as they could," whispers Norma.

I suck in my breath so loudly Sister Michelle thinks I spoke. She pinpoints me with her eyes. "No talking in chapel, Ana!" she says. "Let's take a few moments to send Lizzette's family our thoughts and prayers." We kneel.

"I guess going to Miami is better than going to jail," says Carmen, crossing herself. "But then getting arrested can't be too good—I mean—I don't know what I mean . . ."

We are so thick in thought we don't notice chapel is over until Sister Michelle claps her hands sharply and says, "Ana! Norma! Carmen! Class was dismissed two minutes ago!"

ANA

Later, Norma waits until we are alone to shove something in my hand. "Here, take it. Don't let Carmen see . . ."

"What . . . why . . . ?" Then I look. It's Norma's necklace with the heart pendant. "What . . . ? Why are you giving me this?" I ask.

"We are moving to Miami too," whispers Norma.

"What?"

"My father is afraid he might be arrested."

"But he's a cartoonist!" I say.

"For the wrong newspaper," says Norma. "I want you to have my necklace to remember me by," she adds, folding my hand over the cool metal heart.

We sleepwalk through the rest of the day.

"Has Papi been released?" I ask my mother the minute she picks me up. But then I see her face is white.

"No, but I went to visit him and he was playing cards with that . . . that . . ."

"Who?"

"That Antonio with the pimples who came to arrest him!"

"What!"

"Your father *still* believes Antonio is his *compañero*. He still hopes things will work out!"

I feel my mother and I are in a Cuban snow globe turned upside down.

Fruit Seller

There are strangers in my house. A mother, father, and little girl. The father has a big Adam's apple. Some of the mother's back teeth are missing. The daughter is younger than me, with skin burned dark from the sun, and long hair with tips of gold.

Mami stands up and announces tensely, "Castro has given farmers some control over the land they work. This family has come to stay with us to celebrate." She introduces us. The girl's name is Zulema, and she stares at me.

"Sit and eat," says my mother. Her smile looks like it might crack her face.

We eat. When I see that the man's hands are so swollen he can hardly hold the spoon he prefers to eat with, I think these are the kinds of people my father was talking about.

"Why don't you show Zulema your room?" says Mami when we are done.

Zulema stares at everything. "You have a lot of books," she says, touching them lightly.

"I like to read," I say. "Don't you?"

Her expression tells me she can't read. Now I *know* these are the kinds of people Papi was talking about. I look at her closely to see if there is anything different about people who can't read, to see if there is something dim in their eyes, but the look in this girl's eyes is sharp. Later, after making sleeping arrangments, I drift off, sorting through all the things my father said about *guajiros.*

¡Frutas, naranjas dulces!

I hear that familiar song as Mami and I drag Zulema and her family around the hot plaza. When we see an old family acquaintance and his grandson, Miguel, standing in a bit of shade by a fruit vendor, we rush to them. Getting close, I see he's the same fruit seller and grandson who was at the park when the ice-cream truck exploded! Will the fruit seller and his grandson remember us? Or do we all look alike to them?

"Don Reyes . . ." says my mother, but she corrects herself quickly. "I mean—Comrade Reyes. How are you?"

"I am fine," says Don Reyes, but a tiny flick in his watery-blue eyes tells us he is not in favor of the Revolution and being called *compañero.* "Miguel and I are fine," he adds flatly.

"Hi," says Miguel, chewing on something that glistens in the corner of his mouth. I never liked his fearful look and the way he shoved food into his pudgy face. Ugh!

So I turn to the fruit seller's grandson as Fidel's voice fills the plaza.

"Hola," I say.

"¿Qué tal?" he answers.

"You were at the park when the ice-cream truck exploded,

and sometime before that my father and I bought some fruit from you . . ." I add carefully.

"I remember," he says, flashing me a secret smile. "You were the one with the jeep full of bullet holes! My name is Juan!"

His eyes are as sharp as Zulema's.

"I'm Ana," I say.

But Zulema interrupts us, saying, "I've never seen so many people in one place."

Then Carmen shows up wearing a beret like Fidel's.

"Where's your cigar?" I ask her.

"Ha! Ha! Very funny," she says, looking toward Fidel in the distance as if she is in love. "He is so wise, don't you think?"

My mother looks at me. We are afraid to agree or disagree with anyone about Fidel in public. "How about oranges for everyone?" she says instead.

Fidel's voice fills the plaza as we rip the skin off our fruit. Carmen cheers at everything he says. Chubby Miguel with his light eyes and hair loses himself in his fruit. Zulema narrows her eyes and listens hard. Juan, with his long, strong-looking dark legs, watches warily as he counts the money they've made so far. And then there's me, Ana. Ana—the one with the father in jail.

We eat our oranges as Fidel yells and screams into the microphone. Suddenly, a ripple goes through the crowd. We all look up. A white dove flies around Fidel's head, and suddenly, and maybe because the sun is in our eyes, we think we see the dove poop on Fidel's head! Can it be? Is that what we saw?

ANA

Then, all at once, we burst out laughing like friends who have always laughed together when a bird craps on Fidel's head! When it's time for Zulema to go home, I do a good thing—I give her a book of fairy tales so she could read someday. So my father won't be in jail for nothing.

Death

"School's closed," Carmen gloats at recess. "This is the last day! Sister Michelle said—"

"I know what she said," I say angrily. Sister Michelle had made the announcement that morning. Her stern face looked so sad I wanted to ask her forgiveness for thinking of her as Sister One-Breast. No more school, and Norma not here—now I only had Carmen—whose happy tone made me snap.

"I know what Sister Michelle said," I repeat. "I was in the room."

"What are you so upset about? You knew it was going to happen," says Carmen, as though she's the smartest person in the room. "Catholic schools are closing all over the city. Fidel says religion fools the people—"

"Oh, shut up about Fidel," I say, the rage I feel inside erupting. "They put my father in jail, remember?" Suddenly even Carmen's pretty pink nails bother me.

Carmen stares. "Look, I never wanted to say this—I'm your friend—but maybe your father did something wrong."

"Wrong? Something *wrong*?"

"Or made a mistake, some sort of mistake."

"A mistake? A mistake? I'll tell you who made a mistake— they did. For arresting him. My father fought for the Revolution.

Remember his jeep? The one with at least eighteen bullet holes?"

"I was just saying . . ." she says. "You don't have to get so mad. You are a different person!" she adds.

"So are you," I spit back.

Her mother arrives, and Carmen is just about to jump into the yellow car when my uncle's car drives up behind. "Isn't that your uncle?" says Carmen. "I've never seen him pick you up before." Sudden fear tingling through my spine stops me from punching her. I clutch Norma's necklace around my neck for support, hoping to warm its heart, but it stays cool in my hand. Carmen looks back at me with pity. Her gaze churns my stomach and somehow I know something horrible has happened. The car idles in wait. I break away from Carmen's gaze and run. But inside the car I get no answers from my uncle. His lips are closed tightly. His eyes are open but shuttered in a way that keeps me from looking into them.

"Your mother needs you, " he whispers hoarsely.

Something unspeakable has happened. I grit my teeth all the way home, where I find my grandmother, her mouth open in a shriek, tears tunneling down her powdered face. Mami sits next to her, her face stony as a statue in the park. Mami turns to me and says, "Your father is dead. He had a heart attack." Before I can react, tears crack open her face and it's like an avalanche so violent I lean in to hold her chin, catching, it almost feels like, pieces of her sorrow. She forces her chin down and weeps openly. Then my grandmother grabs Chispa and shoves her crying face into the dog as if Chispa were a pillow, and then they both fall on us, grandmother's rhinestone pin scratching the top of my head. I hold one arm up so I can breathe, even as I pull her to us with my other arm. The aunts and uncles pile onto us too.

"I can't breathe, I can't breathe," I gasp, pulling out from under them. Then I run upstairs into my room with Chispa, who marks my punches in the pillow with her barks.

News travels fast, or slow, I don't know, but soon the house is full of people. Even Miguel, his parents, and his grandfather, Don Reyes with his old, now-extra-watery-blue eyes, show up.

There is a priest. Sister Michelle is there.

There are whispers: "He caught a virus in his heart while fighting in the mountains." "Being in jail made it worse." "That's why he couldn't gain weight." "That's why he died of a heart attack." "The stress was too much for Pedro." "The way things are going in Cuba broke his heart."

No one can eat except for Miguel, his blond hair falling over his fat face as he stuffs it.

"How can you eat?" I say to him with disgust.

He looks bewildered and sad but I don't care. Everyone gets down on their knees, but I go up to my room to throw myself on the bed, hold in my stomach, and rock myself still until I need air, then I go to my window.

That is the first time I see a black car, parking lights on, just idling outside.

Guns

Day by day the family watches the black car that is like an insult to our misery, our grieving, our sadness—until one morning, two men slither out of the car and come to our door. One of them is Antonio Pimple-Face.

"Guns! Where are the guns?" he says.

"Antonio, what are you talking about? Haven't you done enough?" Mami pleads.

"What is the meaning of this?" croaks my grandmother. "There are no guns here!"

Antonio nods to the other policeman, who runs upstairs. I run after him. My aunts and uncles chase after me. To what? To stop him? No—to stand uselessly as I watch him roughly look through my dresser, through Mami's closet. "Stop it!" I scream. "Those are our things!"

The policeman stares. "You have no things! Everything belongs to the state!" Then he pushes us all back downstairs. "No guns upstairs," he announces to Antonio.

"There aren't any guns anywhere," says Mami weakly to them both.

Still—they look through the rest of the house, until they crawl back into their car and drive away. But before we can settle enough to even console each other, another car comes creeping around the corner—to watch.

"It's time to leave Cuba," says Mami solemnly.

"What?" says Grandmother.

"You can't leave Cuba," add the aunts and uncles. "You'll lose everything."

"I don't care," says Mami. "It's a sign—them coming for guns, those cars that watch us—it's time for you, me, and Ana to leave!"

"Why should we leave because of them?" says Grandmother. "They think *everybody* has guns; they watch everybody!"

"Not only because of that—" says Mami. "But because Rafael wanted it so."

"When did he say that?" the family asks.

"Every single time I visited him in jail," says Mami. "Even the day he left this house."

"But Papi told me things would work out . . ." I say weakly.

"What else could he say?" says Mami sharply.

I recoil from the sting of her words. Grandmother leaps in. "I can't leave Cuba. My son is buried here!" she wails, leaning into Chispa, letting my dog absorb her tears.

"When would we come back?" I ask.

"Huh?" my mother responds.

"I said, when would we come back?"

My mother flip-flops like a flounder fish out of water. "Well . . . I guess . . ." She stops and stalls like a car that won't start. "I . . . don't know . . . I mean . . . I am not sure . . ."

ANA

The air gets so heavy she throws in a ray of hope to cut through and lighten it.

"I mean, surely the United States will come in and intervene, and we can come back . . . I don't know . . . I *do* know that as long as that car is out there watching us, we have to leave Cuba."

Grandmother sobs into Chispa as we stand in that place between taking in a breath and letting it out. Or the moment you jump off a diving board, or the moment you wake up gasping and praying your nightmare wasn't real. We stand silent between hoping things will be fine and knowing they will never be the same.

Things *didn't* work out like my father had said. He lied to me. Or he was a fool.

Packing Chispa

My mouth is dry, my armpits wet. My chugging heart beats against my hollow chest. My stomach rumbles for food I don't feel like eating. Yet also, I feel slow, sluggish, and dull as I try to figure out what to take. Leave? Hold? Pack?

It's easy—nothing. The government only allows you to take two outfits out of the country. I don't care, I only care about my drawings, and Chispa.

I help Mami rip a seam in her jacket in which to hide some jewelry. "Do you think Chispa will fit in one of these seams?" I am as fresh and *malcriada* as I possibly can be.

Mami settles back heavily and takes my hand. "*Mija*, I am so sorry. I hadn't even really thought about Chispa. She has to stay, of course, but you must know that she will be fine with the family. In that way, she will always be with us. We will always have family in Cuba, and Chispa is part of that family."

I listen to her foolish Papi-type blather. But at least she's not telling me everything is going to be all right, like he did. And anyway—I knew this was coming. I can see what's right in front of me, even though my father couldn't. I swallow the idea of leaving Chispa in Cuba, like I allow castor oil to slide down my throat when I am sick.

ANA

. . .

In the time of waiting for our papers to come through, my thoughts zip around like flies on stagnant water. Will Sister Michelle go back to France? What does Miguel think about besides stuffing his face with *croquetas*? Is that *guajira* girl, Zulema, and her people happy with what's going on? Is that fruit seller, Juan, still selling oranges? And what about the friends I've lost because of this stupid Revolution, Norma and Carmen?

I think of the things I will leave behind. Will I ever come back for my encyclopedia, my clothes, including the clown costume I wore for Carmen's birthday party? I wonder if Carmen will become a teacher and never get married like she promised that day at the picnic. Thinking of Carmen awakens the nasty rage I feel for her. When did we stop being friends? When my father died? Or when she saw Cuba one way, and I saw it another?

Suddenly I want to finish with her. I grab pencil and paper.

Dear Carmen,

By the time you read this, I will be gone. You must understand, with Papi dead we cannot be in Cuba. We cannot be in a place that loves Fidel Castro. I don't know how we could have let a stupid politician's ideas come between us, but we have.

I write two last sentences.

I hope you find something good in this country.
For now, I do not. Your ex-friend, Ana

I'll mail it from the airport so she'll get it when I'm gone.
The hell with her.

Adiós, Chispa

The day we are to leave is short and confused. One minute, Mami is burning coffee, and the next she is frying fritters. One minute, Mami is giving an aunt a candlestick, or giving an uncle a lace tablecloth, and the next moment she wants them back. The aunts and uncles mill around, bumping into one another.

I put my books and my clothes and some games into a box and tell an aunt to give them to poor children. I make a special box for Chispa. In it, I put a blouse I had worn many times, so it had my smell; my school skirt; and some dog biscuits. That way, Chispa can smell my blouse, sleep on my skirt, and think of me and food.

Then I think of a way of taking Chispa with me. Getting a fresh piece of paper and some paint, I put paint on her paws and make paw prints on the paper. She whimpers, confused.

"It's okay, Chispa," I say, trying to comfort her. "It's okay." Then I wonder if I am lying to her like my father lied to me.

Grandmother comes out of the bathroom with her skirt stuck in her big white panties. The backs of her legs look dimply.

"How funny," she says, rearranging her skirt. But suddenly she collapses into a chair and calls for Chispa. Chispa jumps on Grandmother, leaving paw prints all over her white blouse— but Grandmother doesn't even notice as she buries her face in

Chispa's belly and cries, "I just don't know." Her blouse is getting ruined, and she doesn't even care. Maybe I don't know what to care about either.

"You'll be fine," says an uncle, ignoring the prints on Grandmother's blouse as well. "It's time to go," says an aunt.

Finally it's time to say good-bye to Chispa. I try to wipe her paws clean, wonder why it matters, then crush her to me, letting my tears fall lightly on her head.

"Come, Chispa," says an aunt, tearing her away from me. "In the house until we get back. You are going to live with me now."

"You?" says an uncle, surprised. "I thought I was going to take Chispa!"

The aunt, her face tight with sorrow, shoves Chispa in the house and slams the door shut. "Fine—you can—whatever— let's go!"

Mami trembles while locking the door.

"I'll do it," I say, taking the keys out of her hands and putting them in my pocket. Why does my mother try to lock the house? Once we leave, it will belong to Cuba.

We get into the cars. I'm sure I can hear Chispa ripping at the door with her paws, trying to get out.

Halfway to the airport, I remember I forgot the paw print picture.

Good-byes

The airport lines coil like snakes. We cry. I think Chispa must've scraped her paws bloody against the door by now.

Finally they leave, and as I wonder which aunt or uncle Chispa will love, I look back and see that Grandmother is not with us. She is standing in the distance like a statue, tears making watery lines in her makeup.

"Excuse me, *señora*, please," people plead, moving around her.

"Doña Belén, what is wrong?" Mami cries out as we fight our way back to her.

"I cannot leave," she says tearfully. "I cannot leave Cuba. I am sorry."

"But, Doña Belén . . ." Mami is confused.

People swarm around us.

"I am too old to go someplace new. Cuba is all I have ever known."

"But your son wanted us to leave," begs Mami.

A baby cries in the background.

"No, he wanted *you* and Ana to leave," Grandmother goes on. "I cannot begin again. You and Ana can."

A policeman comes around. "Is there a problem?"

Suddenly I know what to do. "No," I say clearly, staring into

Grandmother's eyes. "You are right, Grandmother, you have to go back and take care of Chispa."

"What? ¿Qué?"

"She is lonely for you," I say slowly. "Look, she left marks all over your blouse."

Grandmother looks at her blouse. "How did that happen?"

"It doesn't matter! She needs you!" I pull the keys out of my pocket. The letter I wrote to Carmen flutters to the ground. Picking it up, I fold the house keys into it. "You'll need these when you go back home and take care of Chispa," I say, pressing the keys and letter into her hand. "And mail this letter to my friend Carmen."

"*Señora*, please move on," yell the passengers behind us. The policeman starts toward us again.

Mami finally jumps in. "Ana is right, Doña Belén."

The policeman is upon us. "What's going on? Move this line! Or . . ."

Grandmother turns to him. "Or what?" she says. "Or what?" She looks as if she will bite his nose off. "What can you do to me that hasn't already been done? What can anybody do to me now that my son is gone? Now no one can ever hurt me again!"

"Please, *señora*," says someone else from behind. "This is no time for television drama."

"Are you joking? This is the perfect time for television drama," says Grandmother dramatically. "I am saying good-bye to my grandchild and daughter-in-law! Shut up!"

Everyone backs off. Grandmother squeezes us good-bye. Then she turns back to the crowd. "Out of my way! Out of my way before I shove this cane—! I must go home! I must *stay* home! I have a dog to take care of and a country to live in! Cuba! Where I belong."

She marches off. Moments later we are faced with the customs agent—it's papi's buddy-boy-pal—Antonio Pimple-Face!

Distraction

"My father gave me that watch," says a young man ahead of us. "Why should I give it to you?" But Antonio takes the boy's watch anyway.

Then Antonio sees us. *"Señora . . ."* he says feebly.

"You betrayed my husband," whispers Mami.

I notice the lump of Mami's jewelry in the hem of her jacket. Antonio will find it unless I do something.

"No!" I say, clutching the necklace at my neck that Norma gave me. "I hope you are not going to take this necklace my great-grandmother gave to me. Haven't you done enough?"

But he looks at Mami. "Look, your husband had a weak heart—"

My mother looks confused, so I jump in, "Don't let them take my necklace, Mami."

"Let me take a look at that necklace," Antonio commands.

I give it to him, hoping he takes it and we can move on.

He handles the pendant, then says, "This is worthless. What's in that briefcase?"

"My drawings!"

"You betrayed my husband," whispers Mami as if she were in a trance.

ANA

I hand him my briefcase. He looks through my drawings quickly.

"Nothing here but children's pictures," he says. "Please go."

Mami and I hurry along to board the airplane—and for the first time I realize, it's just going to be the two of us, from here on out.

Becoming Unglued

On the plane I catch my breath. The stewardess begins speaking English. "Mami, I don't speak English!" I say, feeling another battle coming on.

"Don't worry," says Mami. "They speak Spanish in the United States too." She takes my hand but keeps looking out the window back at Cuba, for as long as she can.

The two of us sleep on and off until we land in New York. I wonder what it'll be like there? But then I know the minute we get off the plane. It's like ice and metal.

A Spanish-speaking customs agent is found to talk to Mami. A short-haired, plain-looking woman wearing a big coat and overalls approaches us. It's Mami's cousin, Mercedes. Mami cries as they hug.

"Hello, Ana," says Mercedes, handing us coats that are too big for us, and suddenly I have a shimmering memory of how lost Papi looked in his own clothes when he got back from the Revolution. The coat hangs on me as we walk to the car, and I am almost too tired and numb to hold it closed. From the back of the car, I listen to them talk about how Fidel changed his tune so quickly, and I remember seeing Fidel in the victory parade so long ago. He looked handsome and strong as a stallion then— now I hope someone gives him a cigar that blows up in his face.

ANA

We drive along a river, and it is as if all color has gone from the world and all that is left is sky and clouds a shade of gray paste. Driving around stuck-together parked cars, we look for a place to squeeze into, and I can't help thinking of the black car creeping around our house in Cuba. Mercedes finally finds a spot, and we walk to a dirty, big brick building with a courtyard.

"Vengan," says Mercedes. "I live in an apartment five flights up." We climb. I am not used to climbing steps—or hot air hitting my face when we enter the apartment. "That heat comes from the radiators," says Mercedes, pointing to metal tanks attached to the floor. In Cuba, heat is everywhere, but here it comes from metal tanks.

To the left of the kitchen is a bathroom and a bedroom. To the right is the tiny living room with a sofa, chair, and television. All along the walls are paintings of big swirls and splotches of gray and black that look like anger.

"Do you like my paintings?" asks Mercedes.

I say yes, but I am not sure.

Mami and I are to share the room off the kitchen, which Mercedes has fixed with a twin bed and a cot. We eat and Mercedes talks about what it's like to be living alongside Puerto Ricans in Manhattan, as Mami talks about Cuba as in a dream. While I eat, my eyes get gummy and heavy and Mami helps me to the small cot in the bedroom. I fall into a kind of sleep and have dreams the color of Mercedes's paintings, and that I am swirling through a gray, gluey sky not knowing where I will land.

Mami

I wake up. Where am I? Small room—Mami is asleep on a bed and I am on a cot. Blinking my eyes, I hear noises—trucks, sirens, then hissing—what was it? The radiator? That's right.

Then I remember: leaving Cuba, Grandmother, Chispa, aunts, uncles, and coming here—where? New York City. Manhattan.

Then the phone rings.

"Lydia," calls Mercedes from the kitchen. "Cuba calling!" Mami stirs. I run out to the phone. From home! Cuba!

"Here, Ana, talk to your grandmother until your mother gets here," says Mercedes.

"Grandmother, how's Chispa!" I gush. "Did you find her okay?" Her voice calms me. I let it slip into my ears and whirl all around. She tells me Chispa is fine, and I can hear her yapping in the background. Tears threaten.

"I am going to make a little bag out of your old school skirt to carry Chispa around in!" says Grandmother. "Chispa will be so happy in it because she can smell you. We will go everywhere together."

Mami comes out of the room, transformed. Her color is pale, her eyebrows sharp with a deep crease between them.

"I am just so tired from the trip I can barely wake up," she says to no one in particular, taking the phone from me.

She and Grandmother talk. I lean in, but too soon the connection is cut as if a knife sliced through it.

"How nice she called right away," says Mercedes. "¿Café?"

"Sí, gracias," says Mami, floating into the living room to look out the window.

"So," says Mercedes, pouring hot milk into a cup of dark coffee. "I suggest you take a few days getting used to being here before you enroll Ana in school."

Mami looks at something way out in the distance. "There's a forest over there," she says. "I thought we were in a city?"

"Oh, that's Inwood Park," says Mercedes before going on. "I said, you should probably take a few days getting used to being here before you enroll Ana in school."

"¿Qué?" My mother's voice is dreamy.

I wonder if Mami has gone deaf. "Mami?" I whisper. "Don't you hear what Mercedes is saying to you?"

"Of course," Mami says suddenly. "School. Yes. Ana must go to school."

"Okay, well, I have to go to work now," says Mercedes. "Here's an extra key—don't lose it and don't open the door to anyone."

"Let's take a walk after breakfast, Mami," I say, trying to keep her attention.

"Ana, I am exhausted. The trip . . . I can hardly keep my eyes open."

"But you just got up . . ."

"*Mija*, please, I just want to close my eyes for a few minutes. We'll have plenty of time to do whatever we have to do tomorrow."

And she disappears into her room.

Bread. Milk. Butter.

The next day, Mercedes is working on her paintings.

She says to Mami, "Why don't you get dressed, go to the corner store, and get me a loaf of bread, a container of milk, and a stick of butter."

Mami's eyes open wide. "Me?"

"Yes, I will go with you," I quickly add.

"*Pero*," my mother protests.

"Don't worry, they speak Spanish in the store," says Mercedes.

"And I remember *inglés* from school—come," I say before Mami can change her mind. Mercedes gives us some money and we go.

At the bodega, I see a girl about my age, skinny with curly black hair around her face. For one second I think it's Carmen! But when I see her face, I see, of course, it's not. This girl's face is like it was held together with tight little lips. "I need one pound of *bacalao*," she says. She gets her dried fish and leaves.

I buy our items quickly and we follow the girl outside. She makes a left turn at our corner. I want to know where she goes. My mother lags, so I pull her along.

"*Hija*, stop pulling!"

Before I know it, all three of us are at our building. The girl uses her key, pushes in, and then stops short, blocking the door. "Are you following me?"

I don't understand what she says. I push the buzzer.

Mercedes's voice comes through the speaker. *"¿Quién?"*

"Ana . . ." I yell into the intercom.

Mercedes rings us in. The girl relaxes, and we all go inside.

"Well, I'm Awilda," says the girl. "You can't be too careful, you know!" Cuban *guaracha* music spills out into the hallway when she opens her door on the third floor.

Someone yells from inside: "Awilda! *¡El bacalao!* Come get money."

The girl dramatically rolls her eyes at us and holds up the bag of *bacalao*. She turns back into her apartment, slamming the door, but it's too late—the musical notes of Cuba hang in the hallway with no one to catch them.

Change

It's time for Mami to enroll me in school. I try to wake her. "Mami, get up. It's time to go almost." She rolls over as though she doesn't recognize me. "Mami, what's wrong! Are you sick?" I put my hand on her brow. Oh God, don't let her be sick!

"*Mija,*" she says, pushing my hand away. "I'm fine. Just tired . . ." And she digs herself farther into the mattress. I call out to Mercedes, who comes in and looks at Mami closely.

"What's the matter with her?" I ask. "A fever?"

Mercedes puts her hand on my shoulder. "I think she's all right," she says carefully.

"But . . ."

"Shhh . . . I'll take you to school," she says finally.

Quietly, we walk to P.S. 189, each waiting for the other to speak. Mercedes goes first. "She's fine," she says lightly. "It'll take her a while to get used to being here . . ."

Then neither one of us speaks until we get to the school and meet the principal, Mr. Simensky. "Welcome!" he says. On his desk are two American flags. I think how in my school in Cuba there are crucifixes everywhere, but here there are American flags everywhere.

Mercedes translates and then adds in Spanish, "Don't

worry. You'll learn English fast. I did! I will pick you up at three o'clock." She leaves, and I'm taken to a classroom.

"Hello," says the young teacher cheerfully. She doesn't look like a nun. Her sleeveless turtleneck sweater accents her breasts. She definitely has two of them.

Every eye is on me. With her hand on my shoulder, the teacher says, "This is Ana, she's from Cuba!"

No one says anything for a long time, until I hear, "I know her, she lives in my building! Hi, Ana!" It's Awilda. "Ana is *mi amiga!*"

Her words are magic. Suddenly everybody knows me too, and after class, I am surrounded by curious faces. I allow myself to forget Mami and let Awilda's friends carry me away into their world.

Mother

I whisper to my mother as she sleeps the days away. I tell her how Awilda shows me around the school saying, "This is my friend Ana. She's Cuban and I'm showing her around." I tell my mother that the lunchroom, gym, and library all smell like chicken feet boiled for hours. I describe all the ways the kids dress because they don't wear uniforms and how different it is going to school with boys. But Mami never says much, even when she barely wakes up.

At school, I begin to understand enough of the half English and half Spanish Awilda speaks to sit with her friends at lunch—Tiffany Santiago, Milagros Pacheco, and Urania Chery. Tiffany and Milagros are Puerto Rican and Urania is Dominican.

"*Me gusta* your hair," says Tiffany.

"And you have pretty eyes," says Milagros before I can answer.

"Do you wear a bra?" asks Urania.

That last question stops me. A bra? "I . . . I don't think I need one yet," I say.

"It don't matter," says Tiffany. "You don't have to *need* one. You can still get a training bra and make believe you need one."

I remember how Carmen and I made fun of Sister Michelle's one breast . . .

"You let the straps show so everybody knows they're growing in," Tiffany continues.

"What school did you go to in Cuba?" asks Urania.

"It was a Catholic school," I say. "The weather is always nice in Cuba, so sometimes we had lunch outside. I had two best friends: Carmen and Norma . . . Carmen looked a little bit like you, Awilda."

"Where are they?" she asks.

I play with Norma's necklace around my neck. "Well, Norma is in Miami . . . she gave me this."

"My mother says that's where all Cubans are going to end up," says Urania, taking a closer look at the pendant. "It's pretty."

"And Carmen . . ." I go on, "Carmen is still in Cuba." The words are not enough to cover my feelings. I blink back tears.

"Does your mother like it here?" asks Tiffany.

And the tears come.

Crazy

One day, I wait for Mercedes to pick me up after school. She's late.

"So, what did you think . . . ?" It's Awilda talking, but I look over her shoulder for Mercedes. I don't see her. I think about my mother being sick.

"What?" I say to Awilda.

"What do you think about doing a *West Side Story* musical recital? My teacher took the whole class to the show. We sat in the back—"

But suddenly this whole scene reminds me of something bad. Awilda's voice sounds like an echo, and something pulls me home . . . I walk . . .

"Hey, wait."

My heart beats so hard I can't hear her.

"Wait a minute."

I walk faster and faster.

"What's up, Ana?"

I break into a run as I replay the bad thing in my mind. It's that last day of school in Havana when my mother didn't pick me up. When my uncle showed up instead . . .

"Wait up, for goodness' sake!" It's Awilda at my heels.

"What's your hurry?" We get to our building. I want to scratch the door open. I see Awilda's mouth moving but hear nothing.

"I'm opening the door as fast as I can!" says Awilda, coming into focus and jamming her key into the lock.

"Hurry up," I say, flying up the stairs. Will I now get home from school in New York City to find my mother . . . ? I burst in the door before I finish the thought.

Mercedes takes one look at me. "She's okay," she says. "But I took her to see my psychiatrist."

I deflate and sit, relieved. But then I shoot up again.

"Why a psychiatrist? Is she crazy?"

"No, but she is anxious . . . and anyway, this is New York City. Everybody goes to a psychiatrist. I have to go pick her up in twenty minutes."

There is nothing more to say. Only everything to feel. Relieved, scared, angry, confused—all those feelings harden like a ball of cement in my chest.

Naming the Painting

The doctor gives my mother sleeping pills. Now my mother sleeps on purpose. But I wait for any moment she is up so I can about to latch onto her, somehow. One day, as I stand outside her door, like a cat waiting for a mouse, Mercedes comes home and begins to paint.

"What are you doing?" says Mercedes.

"Nothing," I say.

"Come on, we don't need two depressed people in the apartment."

"Depressed? Are you depressed too?" I say.

"No, *you* and your mother are."

"I'm not!" I say, angry. "I like school—I made friends!"

"All right! All right!" She pauses before going on. "But it's natural if you feel a little depressed. Funny—it was the opposite with me. I was depressed in Cuba—that's why I came here."

"What do you mean?" I ask.

"Well, my family wanted me to put my art aside and get married and have kids. But I never wanted to do that—so I left."

I think of how my friend Carmen announced she never wanted to get married.

Mercedes goes on, "I wanted to concentrate on my art. I

know you like to draw. Why don't you paint something? You'll feel better."

She hands me some tubes of red and orange paint, a palette, and some brushes. "Paint something cheerful! Clear your mind."

"I don't paint—I draw, with pencils."

"Try something new," she challenges. "Tell you what—make a design with all the beautiful colors of the flowers of Cuba. Here, use this canvas!"

I squeeze some orange paint onto the palette so she'll shut up. Then I squeeze some red paint right next to it.

Before I know it, my hands take over and I make a design that reminds me of my mother, but I don't know why.

Mami stumbles in and sees what I am doing. The colors in my painting seem to wake her up. "Those colors remind me of something . . ." she says, scratching her head. Then it comes to her. "I know—I had a dress that had those colors! It had orange flowers and red flowers!"

"That's right! You wore it on the day we went on a picnic!" I say, locking onto her.

"You made an abstract of your mother!" says Mercedes. "You should give it a name. Call it *Mi mami*."

But now that I've hooked my mother, a mean feeling takes over and I want to see her dangle. "Can I borrow that tube of black paint?" I ask Mercedes. Almost before she's done handing it to me I squeeze some black onto the canvas and smear until the whole thing becomes a muddy brown mess. "That's more like it," I sneer. "*Mi mami*."

My mother stares, then turns, going back into her room.

Tears

But she won't get away this time. I follow her. Mami turns on me. "Your father is gone, and we might never see Cuba again. We have lost everything. Have you forgotten that already? How can you be angry at me for being sad!" She searches around, then shoves a picture in my face. It's the photo of Carmen, Norma, and me on the day we went on a picnic in Papi's full-of-bullet-holes jeep. "Have you forgotten them?"

But I look past the faces of my friends and get a picture in my head more beautiful and important than the black-and-white photo in front of me—Mami, wearing her dress with the orange flowers and red flowers, its skirt flowing around and between my father's legs, as she takes a picture. Papi standing behind her, making faces at us, wiggling his ears, forcing us to smile.

All at once I know, as if for the first time, that something unimaginable has happened—suddenly I can't breathe because in a flash I know my father is dead. He's dead. He died. "Papi is dead, Mami. Papi is dead!" I cry, stunned and unbelieving.

Mami grabs me. And then it's like she can't believe it either. And then we cry, our bodies expanding and deflating with each round of realization.

"And he lied to me! He lied to me!" I cry, hands pressed up against my face.

"Huh? What?" My mother is stunned. She pulls away from me, wrenching my hands from her, and for a moment, we wrestle. She stares me in the face. "What are you talking about?"

"When he said things were going to be all right . . . the day he was arrested," I sob.

My mother grabs me! "He didn't lie to you!"

"He did! He did!" I insist. "And not only that time—when we went for oranges and he made me look closely at the fruit vendor. He told me—he told me there was going to be a new Cuba. He made me believe coming up Cuban was going to be different."

"That wasn't lying," she says passionately. "No! That wasn't lying!"

"What was it, then? What was it?" I cry.

"That was hoping!"

"What?"

"Hoping . . ."

"What do you mean?"

"Yes, he was 'hoping' things would be all right. We all do!"

"But even before that," I say slowly, "when we saw the terrible execution stuff on television—he thought things would turn out all right. He was blind to what was going on.

He wasn't blind to what was going on—he was hoping for it to stop. Don't you see? That's what hoping is," she says slowly, like she's realizing it herself. "To be alive is to hope, you have to keep hoping. No matter what happens, no matter what's in front of you."

And then we stop and let that information wash over us over and over again, like the Caribbean Sea has been hitting the Malecón in Cuba for a long time—and how it will keep caressing and loving Cuba forever.

Mucho Fongs

"Should I cook?" Mami asks suddenly, days later. We have been careful with each other, so I say nothing and put one more dab of paint on my canvas.

But when, out of the corner of my eye, I see her tossing the sleeping pills down the drain, I speak. "Mami! That's a great idea!"

Mercedes, who had been working on a painting right next to me, says, "Sí, perfect! Cook dinner while Ana and I finish up!"

Mami goes into the kitchen but then bursts back into the room. "What am I saying, I don't want to cook! Let's go out to dinner; it's time I saw the neighborhood," she adds brightly. Her smile is beautiful. "Let me put on some makeup," says Mami, running into our room.

"Let's get ready, quick, before she changes her mind," I say.

"I don't think she will," says Mercedes.

Mami comes out. "How do I look?" she says.

"This is New York—nobody cares how you look. But you look great anyway!" says Mercedes.

"Mami—you look so beautiful. I never saw you look so good!" I say, meaning it.

"And I know just the restaurant to go to—Mucho Fongs," says Mercedes.

"Mucho Fongs? What kind of restaurant is that?" asks Mami.

"The best Cuban Chinese food in the neighborhood! Everybody eats at Mucho Fongs!"

We step out the door. The air feels warm; there are leaves desperately trying to grow on the trees.

"I have a new best friend—Awilda," I offer quietly.

Mami blinks and pushes a lock of hair behind my ear. "Remember when you bit your father on the ear?" she says.

"Chispa bit him too."

"I know. You were both protecting me." She smiles. "Tell me about Awilda."

"Well, she's Puerto Rican, and her friends—Tiffany Santiago and Milagros Pacheco—are also from Puerto Rico. And then there's Urania Chery—she's from the Dominican Republic."

"Lots of Caribbean girls . . . just like us," says Mami finally.

"Yes, Tiffany likes my hair."

"Of course. You have beautiful hair. Your father loved it."

"And Urania thinks I need a training bra . . ."

"Training bra?" Mami says, stopping short.

And we allow ourselves to laugh out loud. Just the two of us.

Home

After a dinner of rice and bean egg rolls, we stroll home, stringing thoughts together.

"Papi believed in Fidel Castro, then Fidel broke his heart," I say quietly.

"He did more than that," says Mercedes.

"Awilda is going to be in a musical recital of a show called *West Side Story*. They need a backdrop, and she thinks I should paint it," I say.

"That's a good idea," says Mercedes.

"But I never painted scenery before," I say.

"You never made abstracts or worked with paints before," says Mercedes. "Making a backdrop is like a combination of both!"

Mercedes's idea is so exciting I rush to tell Awilda. I can hear her singing from her apartment as we go up the stairs. "*I want to be in America! Okay by me in America!*' I was practicing my song!" she grins, opening her door.

"I *will* make the backdrop!" I announce.

"Perfect!" says Awilda. "You have to draw a schoolyard and a rooftop—but the most important thing is a fire escape—"

"A fire escape?" I had seen it out our window, but I never thought about it.

"You should go out on yours."

"Out on it?" I repeat dumbly.

"Yeah, believe me, it can be where the most important things happen in life. I never knew that 'til I learned about this play."

I rush to our fire escape the minute we are inside the apartment. "Is it safe?" I ask Mercedes.

"Sure!" she says, helping me step out.

"*¡Muchacha!*" screams my mother.

"It's okay, Lydia," says Mercedes. "Let her step out into the world!"

It feels as if I am weightless and flying through the air.

"Come inside," says Mami, peering through the window.

"You come out, Mami! It's safe! Come and see!"

"One step at a time," Mercedes whispers in my ear. "One step at a time. One step at a time."

Stars

The fire escape becomes my special place to gaze at stars through teary eyes and think about my father and the way he looked that day at the picnic. How he wiggled his ears trying to make us laugh is an image forever seared in my mind.

The fire escape also becomes a place where the stars make me wonder if Norma is meeting cute boys who wiggle their ears in Miami. Or if the Revolution made Miguel lose weight. Or if the *guajiro* girl, Zulema, who came to visit, ever looks at the book I gave her. I even wonder if the fruit vendor and his grandson still sell oranges in Havana, though I can't quite remember the boy's name. Was it Juan? And I have to admit, I even wonder if Carmen ever got my letter.

Suddenly there's a shooting star! I see it clearly. It's so beautiful I stand up and make believe all those people are—at this very moment—looking at the same shooting star, and feeling just as hopeful as me.

The first duty of a man is to think for himself.
—JOSÉ MARTÍ

MIGUEL

MIAMI, FLORIDA · 1961

I am tied to a chair.

"*¡A la una, a las dos y a las tres!*" they cry as they throw me into the pool, chair and all. I hit the water hard and twist my body trying to get out, float up, live, but my hands and feet are tied tight. The cowboys printed on my silk robe sweep up in front of my face, so I can't see my killers. The water rushes through the fabric, into my nose. I can't breathe, and as I sink to the bottom, the echo of the chair peacefully falling into place comforts me.

The pool lights make the water hazy. The sounds of the boys' laughter fade away, and I feel happy and peaceful.

You cannot be afraid if you are dead. Am I? Dead?

Saved

But suddenly, I feel water rushing along my sides, then my head pops out for air. I gasp. Boys who just tried to kill me are giggling and swimming all around, triumphantly lifting the chair, then handing me over to more boys, who pull me up and out of this watery hell. Sputtering, I take a deep breath. My throat is raw.

"*Muchachos*, why are you doing this?" Blinking my eyes, I see it's the priest standing at the edge of the pool. "These pranks . . ."

But Primero, the leader of the gang who threw me in the pool, speaks over him. "I just wanted to welcome him to Florida City Camp, Miami, USA."

"That is not funny, Primero," says the priest. "This is not good. If it wasn't for Osvaldo here, coming to get me, I wouldn't have known this was going on."

The boy standing next to the priest is small and wears glasses.

The priest goes on, "How could I explain this kind of behavior to your parents, who sacrificed so much to send you here to protect you. After Fidel beat back the Americans at the Bay of Pigs mess, anything could've happened. You might've been taken away from them, brainwashed, raised by soldiers somewhere, or forced to got to some Communist country"

"We weren't going to drown him," says Primero. "We just wanted to see if his fat would make him float!" He laughs.

"Primero," says the priest, sighing. "Don't take advantage because you have been here the longest—promise me that these jokes on new arrivals will end! Understand?"

"*Sí, sí,*" says Primero. "I understand."

"Okay, then," says the priest. "Back inside—all of you! And for goodness' sake, untie that boy!"

Primero smacks Osvaldo on the head the minute the priest's back is turned. "This is all your fault, Osvaldo," he says. "I'll get you for this." And he and his gang disappear into the night.

Silently, Osvaldo unties my hands.

"How long have you been here?" I whisper.

"Too long," he replies before slipping away toward the dormitory.

I add my tears to the puddle of water I am left in.

Osvaldo

The next morning, the dim light in the cafeteria soothes my eyes, raw from crying. Still, I see Primero push someone, who bumps into someone else, who bumps into Osvaldo and his tray of food. Osvaldo's tray goes flying as he sprawls on the floor, eyeglasses slipping off and sliding under a table.

"*¿Qué pasó, Osvaldo?*" says Primero innocently. "You're so clumsy!"

Osvaldo lies there as if resting. I find his glasses and hand them to him as the priest enters. "What's going on here?" he demands. Nobody answers. Grabbing a sweet roll, I sneak back to my seat. "More pranks?" he warns.

Everyone shrugs.

"Well, then . . ." He looks around impatiently. "Somebody clean this mess up."

Osvaldo cleans the floor. Primero eats his breakfast as if the mess had nothing to do with him. I chew my sweet roll.

The priest sits next to me. "How are you today, Miguel?"

"Fine," I say, my voice muffled by the roll in my mouth. I hope he leaves me alone.

"Good—you know—it's always rough on new kids when they first get here. The best thing to do is make friends and have fun!" He looks around and announces to everyone, "All of you, have fun, fun, fun today!" His words are like a battle cry, and the boys scramble, tossing their trays onto the counter and racing out the door. In the quiet, the priest looks at me, then follows after them.

Osvaldo and I stay behind as the cook's pots and pans begin to clang and echo in the kitchen. I ask him again.

"How long have you been here?"

"Four months." Then Osvaldo rushes out.

"Four months!" I gasp for air like I had done in the pool. Four months! That can't be! My parents told me I'd be here for just a little while. Just until the Americans got Fidel out of Cuba and things got back to normal. I rush out the door to find Osvaldo—but I'm too late. He's gone. I look into the crowd of kids running here and there in the hazy sun, and it's as if he was swallowed up by the kids or turned into dust and blown away.

Foster Homes

I go back into the lunchroom and grab one more leftover sweet roll. Wrapping it in a napkin, I sneak it back to the dorms, sliding myself along the buildings so nobody sees me. My bed is a mess and I try to tuck and pull the corners here and there, but it's no use. I'll never make my bed as nice as our maid, Grizelda, made my bed in Cuba.

Giving up, I hide the sweet roll under the edge of my pillow cover for later. The dull roar of the boys playing hard outside makes me curl up into a ball. I fall asleep, until I am awakened by voices.

"I feel sorry for that chubby *gordito* new kid."

It was Osvaldo speaking.

"Forget about him—they're getting ready to ship kids off to foster homes," says the other kid. I peek—he's got red hair. He goes on, "Grab your shirt and let's get out of here. I hear they smack you on the head for speaking Spanish in some of these foster homes. Let's go."

I sit up! Foster homes?

The boys leave, and the room feels empty in a different way. I stuff the sweet roll from under my pillow into my mouth before going outside.

The sizzling sun makes me look for shade where I can sit,

away from the boys by the pool, who shove and push—playing so hard they must leave marks on one another's bodies. I wonder if I should hide, like Osvaldo and his friend? Nobody told me about foster homes.

Leaning against a shady spot on the wall, I sink down, put my head between my knees, and let the snot and tears come. I've got to call my parents.

Phone Call Number One

When the three-minute call to Cuba finally goes through, I choke.

"What's wrong?" says my father. "Why are you crying? Calm down, son, *cálmate*."

"I can't," I weep. "I'm afraid of being sent to a foster home . . ." Then I babble, "I thought the Americans were going to make everything right in Cuba again . . . and I was going to come home . . ."

"Stop crying, I can't understand you if you cry. Calm down!" pleads my father.

I try, but I can't stop the snot and tears from flowing. I hear my mother in the background.

"Your mother wants to know if you're eating."

"*Sí,*" I whisper. I decide to forget about Americans saving us and ask about what really scares me. "But what about the foster homes?"

"Look," says Papi. "I never heard anything about foster homes! Anyway, just do what they tell you. You are in a good church organization."

I swallow my sobs, hear my father sigh, and imagine them on our patio in Cuba. The sun bleaching one end of the table as they sit under a shady umbrella at the other end. Grizelda bringing them *café*—if I were there, she would be bringing me a hot chocolate. She'd pat my cheek with brown hands warmed by the cup she was holding, her bracelets tinkling around her wrists. Then she would offer me a sweet roll. That's when we'd hear the Black street vendor singing *¡Frutas, naranjas dulces!* coming up the street. And Grizelda would let down a basket of money, on a string, and the fruit seller's helper would take the money and send up fruit. Oh, this was too much!

Grizelda always took care of me. She had a family and children somewhere in the mountains, but she lived with us and always took care of me. I wish she could take care of me now.

I chance talking. "I want to come home. When can I come home?"

"You can't come home!" says Papi. "This is not a good place to be."

Then my mother gets on the phone. *"Hijo . . ."* she says. "We miss you. Don't forget to eat."

The sound of her voice weakens whatever is holding me together. The click of the phone going dead puts an end to me, and I sink into myself. There's only one other thing to do.

Hide out with Osvaldo and his friend, the red-haired kid.

Escape

It takes me days to find them. They are never with the boys throwing balls at one another's heads, or knocking one another down, or wrestling, or trying to high dive into the pool from a wobbly ladder held by no one.

Finally one day when I'm on the far side of the fence that keeps us in, licking the inside of a cookie clean, I see Osvaldo looking for something along the ground.

"Hey," he says.

"Hey," I say, quickly stuffing the soggy remains into my mouth.

"Tell me if you see anyone coming, okay?" he says.

"Okay. But what are you looking for?" I say.

"Just tell me if you see anyone coming," he repeats.

I look up. "Your red-haired friend is coming."

Osvaldo peers into the distance. "Oh, that's Cómico. He's all right. He's the one who told me about this ditch."

"Glad you didn't get drowned," Cómico says to me when he joins us. "Primero and his gang didn't tie me to the chair when I first got here. They just threw me in the pool and held my head underwater. You got special treatment." He smiles, holding out his hand. His grin is so big I can almost see the teeth in the back of his mouth. "I am Luis Jiménez—but you can call me Cómico."

"Miguel Reyes," I say, taking it.

"Found it," says Osvaldo, suddenly pointing.

"Good job, Osvaldo!" Osvaldo has found a groove in the loose dirt that goes under the fence. It looks deep enough so you could wiggle through to get to the other side.

"Let's go," says Cómico. And he slips into the ditch, feet first, wiggling under the fence until he crosses over.

Osvaldo slips in after him. Once on the other side, he turns to me and says, "Coming?"

I pause. "Are we escaping?"

"Just for the day," laughs Cómico.

"But won't the priest get mad at us for leaving?" I ask.

"He won't even know we're gone," says Cómico.

"But where are we going?"

"To make some money," says Cómico.

"Why?" I ask. I never made money in my life.

"For Cuba!" they answer.

"How?" I ask.

"Tomatoes!" says Cómico.

"Come on," says Osvaldo.

The screams and grunts from the boys violently playing in the distance make my mind up for me. I cross myself, in the name of the Father and the Son and the Holy Ghost—and slip into the trench after Cómico and Osvaldo.

Cómico

But my belly gets in the way.

"Suck it in," says Cómico.

I suck in my stomach and keep going until I feel the sting of the fence as it cuts me. I try to wiggle through even faster!

"Slow down!" says Cómico.

A sour cookie-cream taste comes up my throat.

"Just be still," says Cómico. "It's just a scratch. Don't move. Here, let me untangle your shirt."

I feel like a stuck pig.

"Now just keep coming . . . slowly," says Cómico.

When the fattest part of me gets through, the rest is easy.

"You did it!" they cheer, patting me on the back.

I turn away and keep brushing the dirt off my clothes long after the dirt is gone so Osvaldo and Cómico can't see my face.

"You did good," says Cómico. When I don't look at him, he adds, "I have to take a pee," and walks into some reeds. Suddenly he screams, "Help! There's a scorpion attached to my pee-pee! Help!" We run toward him as he turns to us, laughing and waving his pee-pee around. "Ha-ha! Just kidding. Now, come on! Time to make some money!"

We get to a clearing where I see rows and rows of tomatoes, and dark-skinned families of pickers wearing straw hats.

"Are those Cubans?" I ask.

"No, I think *mejicanos* and Puerto Ricans. Come on," he says. "I have been doing this for weeks."

We walk up to a run-down shack where an *americano* man gives us each a basket.

Cómico shows me how to pick the tomatoes so they don't get bruised. It looks easy, but it is wicked hard, with tiny thorns getting under our nails and the sun beating down on our heads and shoulders.

At the end of the day, we split the money three ways and find a shady place to rest. I sneak a look at my two new friends and want to talk—but I don't want to interrupt in case they are daydreaming of Cuba.

Money

"Why can't you brainwash a Cuban?" says Cómico. Then he says, "Because he's too busy talking crap to listen!"

I don't understand his joke. "But all Cubans don't talk crap," I say. "My grandfather talks to his blue Ford when it won't start, but that's not really talking crap—and once at a rally, when everybody made jokes about Americans, he told me it's not right to make jokes about whole groups of people—so that goes for us Cubans too, doesn't it?"

"Oh, come on," Cómico says, eyes bugging out. "I know that! The reason I'm cracking that joke is that we are here because our parents thought we could be brainwashed into thinking like Fidel. Get it?" When I don't answer he goes on desperately. "How about this one—how come Cubans do so much talking in the street?" He answers his own question. "Because since Fidel took over the telephone company, it's getting harder and harder to make a phone call. Get it? Get it?" Then he bends over laughing so hard tears come to his eyes, forcing him to twist away.

That's when I think that what he's saying has nothing to do with brains, or washing, or talking crap. It has to do with trying to laugh instead of cry, trying to smile instead of frown, trying to keep going instead of giving up. The more I think of it, the more right it feels. Cómico makes jokes to somehow keep

Fidel away. To actually be stronger than Fidel. To rise past him. Cómico turns back to us, his eyes hurt and red.

"Let's go back," says Osvaldo quietly.

"Yes," I say, "I'm hungry."

"Okay," whispers Cómico.

Crawling back under the fence into the camp is easy. The killer games are over, and the boys are inside getting ready for dinner.

"How many Cubans does it take to make money?" asks Cómico quietly. Then he answers his own question. "I'll tell you— one Cuban—me—because I am going to pick as many tomatoes as I can, to make enough money so I can buy airplane tickets for my parents to come to Miami and be with me again—and the hell with Fidel."

I hear muffled voices, and knives and forks scraping plates, coming from the dining room. There are pink and purplish streaks of light all through the sky. "What does that sky remind you of?" I ask.

"Looks like a Cuban sky to me," says Osvaldo. "We are so close to Cuba—I'm sure people there right now are looking at this exact sky."

"Yes," agrees Cómico. "We are less than a hundred miles away. A hundred miles is nothing in America. I heard Americans out west drive one hundred miles to go for ice cream!"

We three stop and stare, and I feel we all want to reach up to grab a firm piece of sky and swing on home to Cuba—but instead we fall into step back to the dorms.

Nervous Breakdown

The more boys crowd into the camp, the more alone I feel. The new boys cry louder than the old boys, and I am just falling asleep to a symphony of loud and quiet tears when one wail cuts through like a knife.

The lights go on; fifteen boys jump out of bed and follow the scream. I bump into Osvaldo and Cómico. Our eyes widen as the scream begins to sound like a cat being electrocuted. It's Primero. We find him in the middle of his bed, clutching his blanket to his chest (he had breasts!), his little black eyes looking around wildly. Still—I can't help notice the cross and gold chain around his neck and wonder how he got it past customs in Cuba.

"I want to go home! I want to go home! I want my *mamá!*" he cries like a baby.

The priest enters, shoos us away, and sits by Primero's bed, saying, "*Cálmate.*"

"I want to go back to Cuba," Primero wails. "I want to see my mother and father and I want to sleep in my old room. How could my parents have left me here?"

"Now, now," says the priest. "Your parents are doing very important work fighting Fidel."

"That's because they love Cuba more than they love me," cries Primero.

"Don't say that—they sent you here for your own safety." Then the priest looks up sharply at us. "Go back to your beds— all of you!"

"I thought Primero was such a tough guy," says Cómico, cursing in amazement.

"He doesn't look so tough now," says Osvaldo.

"I know how he feels," I say.

"Are you on Primero's side or something?" says Cómico.

"No, I'm not taking his side," I say. "He almost drowned me, remember? I'm just saying that . . . Never mind."

"What?"

"Nothing. It's just that . . . everybody cries."

"All right, all right," says Cómico. "But we have to be brave, like our parents say. Or the three of us would be crying like Primero. We would be going, wah, wah, wah. ¡Mamá! ¡Mamá! Wah! Wah! Wah! *Dame un besito* and change my diaper while you're at it." Cómico runs around like a baby rubbing his eyes.

"Can parents love Cuba more than they love us?" says Osvaldo quietly.

"No," says Cómico savagely. "The fact that they sent us here proves that they love us more! Don't you know anything?"

The next day Primero is gone.

Beca

"What happened to Primero?" I ask Cómico on our way to the fence.

"He got a *beca*," says Cómico sarcastically over his shoulder.

"*¿Beca?*" I say. "He got a scholarship?"

"No!" Cómico stops and looks at me as though I am stupid. "It's what they call sending you to a foster home.

The very thought of a foster home shoots fear and anxiety into my bones.

"There's going to be a lot of *becas*," he adds. "This place is getting so filled up, we're going to have to share toilet paper soon. Or eat our own poop. Hey, maybe that's how the word *comemierda* was made up!"

"Stop," says Osvaldo.

"Okay, how many Cuban butts will one piece of toilet paper wipe?"

I feel like throwing up.

"They have to put us somewhere!" says Osvaldo, ignoring Cómico's disgusting joke.

"But where are the foster homes?" I ask, feeling sicker and sicker.

"All over America! Some kids get sent to Idaho, where the potatoes come from, or Chicago, Illinois, where all the gangsters like Al Capone are. Some even go to Washington State, where it's almost Canada and gets so cold your pee turns to ice before it hits the ground!"

Cómico finds the ditch, and we slip under the fence quickly and quietly. We march to the tomato farm fast. Then, hardly speaking, we pick the tomatoes, not even caring if we bruise them.

We split our money without saying a word. Then Osvaldo catches a lizard and kills it. Then Cómico finds a rock and beats the ground until it catches his finger. He howls in pain even as he throws the rock into the bushes.

"We have to stick together," he says seriously.

"*Sí*," says Osvaldo. "Remember, our parents sent us here because they love us so much."

"Sometimes I wish they loved us less . . ." says Cómico quietly.

For once, he's not joking.

Tossed Away

Weeks later, we are in the cafeteria eating grilled cheese sandwiches and some slimy green vegetable when the priest makes an announcement.

"As you know, it's been getting a little crowded around here. So, you'll be happy to hear that *four* of you are getting the opportunity to give up your places for others. You are: Jorge Aguirre, Emilio Delgado, Jordan Falcón, and Miguel Reyes. Congratulations, *beca* winners."

He said my name. Cómico looks at me quickly. "If I were you, I'd sneak out under the fence and run away!"

"No, you wouldn't," says Osvaldo. "How would your parents ever find you if you did that?"

"If I called your name, come see me at the office after lunch," adds the priest, leaving the room.

"Maybe your foster home won't be too far," says Osvaldo. "Maybe you'll have your own room and the family will have a swimming pool and a football field—they love football in the United States. It's like a religion."

The cheese in my sandwich sticks to the roof of my mouth. Cómico explodes. "It's all Fidel's fault!" he cries out. "This is . . . crazy."

I try to unstick the cheese with my middle finger.

"I know," says Osvaldo. "But all this is happening for a reason."

The cheese plops down in my mouth like mold. Cómico cries out, "There is no reason. We are just Cubans flying through space—you know, I heard the newspapers call sending us kids here 'Operation Pedro Pan.' And you want to know why—because we're flying through the air, like Peter Pan, landing in *Neverland*, wherever the hell that is!"

Suddenly what he is saying seems so funny it makes me laugh—so hard the cheese pops out altogether. And then I keep laughing like I'll never stop.

The priest comes looking for me. "Miguel? Are you all right?"

I suck up the slimy green vegetables.

"Maybe you should—wait a minute . . . stop eating . . ." says the priest, squinting at me.

But why should I stop eating? I need to eat so I can fly through space (or drown in pools). Ha-ha! Tears from laughing run down my cheeks, slip into my mouth, and I suck them down my throat too! Yum! Tasty!

"Calm down, calm down, Miguel," says the priest again, seriously. "You are having a nervous, hysterical reaction. Come with me, come with me, you can relax in my office."

He helps me into his office because I am doubled over with laughter. Still—I can't help turning and waving good-bye to Cómico and Osvaldo. "*¡Adiós, muchachos!*"

"Drink this." The priest offers me water once we get inside.

Giggling, I drink the water, spilling half of it on the floor.

"That's it, calm down, Miguel. Calm down."

Then it is as if something grabs me from the inside and twists out sobs that stick my eyelashes together.

"That's better. Much, much better," says the priest, shaking his head from side to side. "Get it out, get it all out."

Adiós

I make a not-funny joke to myself as I pack, a week after I get the news I'm leaving.

Why is crying good?

Crying is good because it feels so good to stop.

I hold up the cowboy robe I almost got drowned in. The pool water made it shrink, so I leave it on my bed. Maybe it'll fit the next kid coming up from Cuba.

The priest sticks his head in the door. "I will bring the car around and take you to the station," he says. "You'll have a fine time in New York City," he adds. "It'll be a long train ride, but it will be worth it!"

I wait until he is gone before I eat the sticky bun I had saved from breakfast. It is sweet and thick and makes me feel good for as long as it is in my mouth. My friends come by to say good-bye.

Cómico hands me a bag. "Some desserts for you," he says.

"Thanks," I say. "And thanks again for saving me from drowning."

He just shrugs and shakes my hand, and then he pats me on the shoulder.

"I think you lost weight, man," says Cómico.

I am surprised. "Me?" I say, looking down on my stomach. "Really?"

"No," he says seriously.

We laugh. Then we don't say anything for a minute.

Finally Cómico says, "I have a farewell joke. You know how come Superman couldn't fly off the Malecón in Cuba?"

"Because there was kryptonite nearby?" I say.

"No, because the whole country was holding on to his cape trying to fly away with him."

But that idea makes me feel sad. What's to become of Cuba if all Cubans do is fly away?

"What's the matter?" says Cómico. "You look like dog *caca* all of a sudden!"

"No, he doesn't," says Osvaldo.

"You're right. He doesn't look like dog *caca*," Cómico agrees. "He looks like dog *caca* on a hot summer day!"

We stand quietly until Cómico says, "How many Cubans does it take to say good-bye?" Osvaldo and I just stand there waiting for Cómico's punchline. "None," he says, "because we are not saying good-bye, we are saying, 'See you later. *Hasta luego.*'"

Shaking hands, we hear a car beep. It's the priest. With one last look back to me, Cómico and Osvaldo turn away and get absorbed by a crowd of boys passing by.

I stuff my things into my bag, even as I stuff my feelings down into my throat, wondering where I will land.

Pennsylvania Station

I am in Pennsylvania Station in New York City.

"Excuse me, excuse me," people say, because I am in their way no matter where I stand! My back and arms ache as I pull out the note the priest had given me. It says I have to find a place called Nedick's by the entrance on the street level. I walk up and up, following the cold air that crawls down my neck as bundled-up people hurry around, not looking into one another's eyes. How do they not collide? Checking my note again, I find Nedick's and wait, watching an old woman beg for money. I also see a man falling asleep on his feet. The buses and taxis swoosh by when suddenly, out of nowhere, someone taps me on the back. I turn, my heart in my mouth—

"Hey, steady—*tranquilo, tranquilo* . . ." says a young man with longish hair, wearing jeans. "Are you Miguel Reyes?" he asks.

I catch my breath. He knows me! But who is *he*? "*Sí*," I say.

"I am so happy that you are here," he says in Spanish with a thick American accent. "I am Father Fitzgerald. Call me Father Fitz."

He's a priest? He doesn't look like a priest!

"*Ven*," he says. Then he rushes me into a tunnel he calls the subway.

A train rumbles toward us! We shove in. I see a deaf man

making signals with his hands and selling whistles. I see a woman with toes sticking out of her shoes carrying four big paper bags.

We get off the subway and go outside, where even colder air cracks my face. Then we get on a ferry boat. I am confused! I thought I already was in New York City? "Where are we going?" I ask. "Why are we on a ferry?"

"Staten Island *is* in New York City. Just not attached to it," says Father Fitz. On the ferry I think of crossing Havana Harbor in Cuba with my grandfather and throwing coins into the water for the poor kids to catch.

The ferry pulls away from the skyline as I give up trying to understand. I head inside the boat in search of warmth when I see *La Estatua de la Libertad*. "That is the Statue of Liberty," I point out, amazed. I had seen it in pictures in schoolbooks, but it is different seeing it for real.

"Yes," says the priest. Then he recites, "*Give me your tired, your poor, your huddled masses yearning to breathe free, the wretched refuse of your teeming shore. Send these, the homeless, tempest-tost to me. I lift my lamp beside the golden door!* T-o-s-t means tossed."

"*Sí*," I say. "I know what is written on her bottom."

"Actually, it is written on the bottom *part* of the statue."

Sí, I think—whatever. But I'm not one of those people who were "wretched" or "homeless" or "tempest-tost."

Am I?

Tottenville

We rush through the St. George Terminal in Staten Island and find a diner nearby. The waitress gives us hamburgers and fries and Cokes. I eat until my plate is clean and the glass empty, and in that way—stuffed with food and drink—we get to the van. There, we hunch over, waiting for it to warm up.

My eyes get heavy as we drive off, and in the fake warmth of the car I fall asleep, wondering if people ever used their car heaters in Havana. I don't wake up until the priest says, "Here we are, Miguel! Welcome to Tottenville!"

I am in a world of black trees with bare branches ready to reach out and grab me. What is this place? Where am I? In a city? The countryside? A town? We drive up to a cathedral or church with huge red doors. The gate mysteriously opens, and the van drives in. The hairs on the back of my neck rise to attention.

"Welcome to the Mission of the Immaculate Virgin, Miguel," says the priest. "You are in Mount Loretto, Staten Island, where you will be joining orphans from all over the city."

"Orphans?" I croak in broken English. "Orphans? I am not an orphan. Orphans are kids without parents. I have parents!"

"Don't worry, Miguel—the director will answer all your questions," says Father cheerfully.

The place smells like chicken soup and pine. I meet the

director, Mr. Sherman, a short, thick man with a bullet-shaped head. There are two small American flags on his desk, but no pictures of the Immaculate Virgin the place is named for.

He looks at me carefully. "Greetings, Miguel—"

"*Señor,*" I interrupt. "There must be a mistake. I am not an orphan."

His eyes narrow. "Of course not, Miguel," he says. "No, no, no, don't worry. You won't be with the orphans and the others here. We have a special place for you refugees."

Refugee? Was I a refugee? Did that mean I was "wretched" or "homeless" or "tempest-tost" after all?

"And you won't have to go to school with the others either. You Cubans can go to public school off campus!" The director goes on, "You'll get along just fine. Besides, you'll only be here temporarily."

"I have to call home . . ." I say.

"Of course."

"But—"

"Now grab your bag and let's go." I look to Father Fitz for help, but he is gone.

I grab my bag and follow Mr. Sherman.

Refugees

I see a phone booth down the long, waxy hallway. "I have to call home . . ."

"Tomorrow," says Mr. Sherman in a way that shuts me up and makes my heart sink.

And then—my heart hits rock bottom—when I hear the murderous sounds of boys playing in a gym. Through the door's window I see boys throwing basketballs at one another's heads.

"Don't worry, you won't have to play with them," says Mr. Sherman.

But I hold my breath until Mr. Sherman leads me to a small dorm where the smiles of eight Cuban boys hit me like warm sun. I let my breath out.

"Here's the Cuban section," announces the director. "You'll bunk here with other refugees like you! Boys—this is Miguel Reyes."

The boys stare, frozen—but the minute Mr. Sherman slips out the door they swarm and seep around me, pumping me for information. "¡Hombre! *How did you get here? Where were you before? Where did you live in Cuba? How old are you?*" "*What have you heard from home?*"

Finally, one tall boy with black hair that falls over his eyes says, "¡*Cálmense, muchachos!* Give him a chance to breathe."

They do what he says. He sticks out his hand. "Nelson Ayala," he says.

I shake it hard, take a deep breath, then ask, "Who are those boys playing basketball . . . ?"

"Oh . . . those are the orphans and delinquents who live here," says Nelson.

"Delinquents?" I ask.

"Bad kids in trouble with the law," he answers.

"Mr. Sherman said we won't be playing with them—" I start.

"Or do anything else with them," says Nelson.

I am relieved for a moment, then ask, "Is there a pool around here?"

"Are you kidding? No!" says Nelson. "Take that bed," he adds, pointing to a disheveled mess in a corner.

As I try to straighten it out, I spy a bag of chips on somebody's dresser. "Anybody eating those?" I ask.

Nelson tosses it to me, and I examine it, thinking . . .

"We'll be fine as long as we stick together," he says.

"Yes, but there are more of those delinquents than there are of us," I say slowly.

All sets of eyes flicker at one another before turning away.

I stuff my face with chips.

Cat Eyes

Nelson waits outside the phone booth, and I am just starting to dial when three boys appear. One has brown curly hair, another has black straight hair, but it's the one with the big, frizzy yellow hair, big hands, and cat eyes who bangs on the door. "You—on the phone," he growls.

I squeak open the door and step out. "Hi, my name is Miguel Reyes. I was just trying to call Cuba."

"What's the matter?" he asks.

I look at Nelson, who keeps fooling with his book bag. "What do you mean?" I say.

"I said, what's the matter? Why are you calling Cuba?" he hisses. "Are you complaining your rooms aren't nice and special enough?" His yellow cat eyes glint. His tobacco breath smacks my face.

"No, I wasn't complaining," I say, sucking in my stomach. "I was just . . . er . . . saying hello to my parents. Do you call your parents sometimes?"

"No!" he says flatly.

His friends look both ways. Out of the corner of my eye, I see Nelson tightening up the strap on his bag. "How's the library here?" I ask. "I haven't been yet. We were just on our way . . ."

"How should I know how the library is? I don't go there!" Cat Eyes answers.

All at once, the boys rush us, but Nelson, just as quickly, swings his book bag at their heads!

"Whoa," says the boy, his cat eyes round with surprise.

But Nelson keeps swinging his bag at them like a crazy person. "This is as close as you are ever going to get to a book, Cat Eyes!"

Mr. Sherman barrels down the hallway.

"What's going on here? Break it up!" he yells. "Attention!"

"They started it," says Nelson, putting down the bag.

"What happened?" Mr. Sherman demands.

"I was trying to call Cuba," I say.

"Next time use the phone in my office!" he barks. "Go back to your rooms!"

Nelson and I turn away, but Mr. Sherman shouts, "And you three, give me twenty push-ups! On the double!"

"What?!" says Cat Eyes. "How come the Cubans get to go to their room and we get to give you twenty push-ups? That's not fair!"

"These Cuban refugees are guests in our country," says Mr. Sherman. "Guests!"

"So, what are we?" says Cat Eyes.

"You are the three smart alecks who are going to give me twenty push-ups! Now!" says Mr. Sherman more sternly.

The boys drop to the floor and begin doing push-ups, grumbling, "This is not fair."

"Come on." Nelson pulls me away saying, "That's Cat Eyes. He's the one to stay away from."

"I don't have to stay away from him because I'm getting out of here," I say.

"What?" says Nelson, confused.

"Just as soon as I call home."

Phone Call Number Two

"*¿Papi?*"

I signal to Nelson that I got through.

"*¿Hijo?*"

Nelson holds up three fingers, telling me I have three minutes!

"*Papi*, I don't have much time. Things are getting worse!"

"How did you know!"

"Huh?"

Papi lowers his voice. "Fidel is cracking down. Last week a bomb went off at a department store right in the heart of Havana." He pauses. "You're never coming home."

"*¿Qué?*" I choke.

"We decided to join you in the United States."

"*¿Qué?*"

"Just your mother and I—your grandfather will stay, stubborn old man!"

"But . . ."

"He is old and sometimes I think he just won't leave his blue Ford behind." He rambles on . . . "Listen . . . we just don't know when we will get there . . . it's not easy getting visas. The lines are long. Many people want to get out. We should've left when your friend Ana and her mother left a year ago."

"Ana wasn't really my friend . . . She never really liked me." I remember the way she looked at me the day the dove crapped on Fidel's head at the rally and then when her father died—she was even mad at me for eating.

"You know who I am talking about!" he snaps, but then switches from impatient to worried. "How are you?" The fear in his voice knocks me out.

"I am in an orphanage . . ." I say weakly.

"Yes, I know," says Papi. "Thank goodness!"

He knows! "How can you let me be here?" I ask.

Nelson fools with Mr. Sherman's American flags, but I can tell he is listening.

"This place is full of juvenile delinquents," I continue.

"But Catholic Charities told me they kept you *cubanos* separately," says my father.

"They do!"

"So, what's the problem?"

"I . . . The other kids think . . . I don't know . . . they just don't like us . . ." How could I explain?

"Just take care of yourself. Make the best of it!" he says impatiently.

"But what can I do?" I feel him slipping away.

"For God's sake, Miguel—I just told you—things are getting worse here in Cuba. We have to leave our house, car, books, everything we own behind. Your grandfather won't leave, the family is breaking up—can't you figure out how to take care of yourself at a kids' camp for at least a little while—"

There is a click, and the line is dead.

"I can't believe it," I say to Nelson. "He told me to figure it out! I . . . I . . ."

Nelson shrugs his shoulder. "You have to understand they are far away," he says. "They don't know what it's like here in America. Besides, they have their own problems now. Big ones dealing with that *comemierda de Fidel Castro*."

Back in our room, Nelson waves a fresh bag of potato chips in front of my face. "Miguel, Miguel, want some chips?"

But I don't hear him.

"Miguel, what's the matter?"

"Huh?"

"Chips, man. Do you want these chips? Where was your mind, Miguel? You look like you were a million miles away."

But I wasn't a million miles away. Now I was probably more than 1,000 miles away, from Cuba, where my father just said, *". . . can't you figure out how to take care of yourself at a kids' camp for at least a little while?"*

And then I hatch a plan . . .

Separation

"¿Qué? ¿Qué?" says everyone in the room. "Are you crazy, Miguel?"

I swallow hard. "No, Nelson, it's the only way. Listen to me— we are already separated from home, our parents, and all our friends, right?"

"Yeah, so, we have to stick together," Nelson insists.

"Are we sticking together or hiding together?" I ask.

"But bunking with those delinquents? I don't know. They're wild and crazy," says Nelson.

"They're crazy? You were pretty crazy yourself, swinging that book bag around," I say.

"They're still not like us. We're different," says Nelson, defending himself.

The rest of the boys agree.

"How?" I ask.

"We are not delinquents. And we have parents," Nelson adds quietly.

"And that is exactly how we are like them!" I say.

"What?" Everybody sings out like a shocked chorus.

"We have parents who are not here," I repeat. "And *they* have or had parents who are not here." No one says anything, so I push through. "Just sticking together as Cubans doesn't work if we are sticking together alone."

"But sleeping in the same room with them?" exclaims Nelson, his eyes bugging out.

"Yes," I say. When nobody says anything, I know I am right.

Zip Gun

Bags packed, the Cuban boys and I walk to the delinquent dorm as though we are walking off a plank. Getting there, we quickly look around. Everyone is around Cat Eyes's bed except for a Black boy, who is reading on his own bed.

"Attention!" says Mr. Sherman.

The boys around Cat Eyes stand up like shots.

"These Cuban boys have decided to move in with you," says Mr. Sherman, rolling his eyes. "Get along. That's an order!" He leaves.

The Black boy goes back to his reading, but the ones who were standing around Cat Eyes's bed quickly turn back to him—suddenly there is a snap, and a scream of pain.

"Oh no . . ." says one kid. "That popped like a gun in a movie. You got big troubles now."

"Shut up," says Cat Eyes, his tough voice quivering.

The boy reading drops his book and rushes over. "There's blood!"

"Thanks for telling me, Julius," says Cat Eyes sarcastically. "You are a genius."

"You better clean that up before Mr. Sherman comes back," the boy named Julius says, running to the door.

It's like they have forgotten about us Cubans, so we go over for a look. Cat Eyes is clutching his bleeding hand to his chest. On the bed is a car antenna, a piece of wood, and some rubber bands.

"What's the matter, you never saw a zip gun before?" he says, trying to sound tough, but I can see tears hanging from his golden eyelashes.

"A . . . zip gun?" I look at the things on his bed. It doesn't look like a gun, but it must've worked because it made a tiny hole in Cat Eyes's hand. "No, I never saw a zip gun before," I say.

Then we hear footsteps.

"Mr. Sherman is coming!" says Julius. "Now we're *all* going to be in trouble!"

There's a tight moment of panic. Then, as Mr. Sherman comes in, and even before I know what I am doing, I run toward him clutching my side. "*¡Ay, el apéndice!*" I cry. "*¡El apéndice!*"

"Miguel! What's wrong?" asks Mr. Sherman, confused.

"*¡Tengo apendicitis!*" I say, doubling over.

"Appendicitis? You think you are having an appendicitis attack?"

"*Sí*, yes," I cry out.

"Come, come," he says, worried. "Let's go to the nurse's office immediately."

He rushes me to the nurse's office, where I lie on a cot, twisting and turning in fake pain until the nurse calls an ambulance. Mr. Sherman rides to the hospital with me, hovering nervously all the way.

When the doctor examines me, I make believe I am feeling better and better by the minute. "I guess maybe it was just gas," I finally say in broken English. "I feel okay now."

By the time Mr. Sherman and I get back, Cat Eyes had hidden the zip gun, bandaged his hand, and put on a shirt with cuffs big enough to cover it. I walk in, and the boys stare. As soon as they are sure Mr. Sherman is gone, the delinquents crowd around me. Cat Eyes waits, then says, "You did good."

I let go of a breath I didn't know I was holding.

Friends

Cat Eyes and I have laundry duty. I make sure there's a pile of towels between us for protection—just in case he suddenly feels like punching me in the nose or something when I ask him this question.

"Hey, Cat Eyes, why did you make a zip gun?"

His face gets tight. "Because I'm going to shoot my stepfather in the butt first chance I get."

I am shocked. Shoot his stepfather in the butt? I cannot imagine wanting to shoot my father in the butt. I can't even *imagine* my father's butt! But I ask anyway. "Why?"

Cat Eyes looks at me as if I am the stupidest person in the world. "Because he hits my mother."

Suddenly he pushes his fist in his eye to stop a tear. "Man, oh man, I really hate when I feel like this." Snot starts running out of his nose. I hand him a towel.

"Doesn't your father hit *your* mother?" he asks, wiping his face. I have to laugh. "No," I say. "I mean, they disagree. He had to convince her to send me here to the United States."

He squints as if something new occurred to him. "Yeah, so what's up with you Cubans coming over here?"

I tell him how Cuban kids were sent to the United States

under Operation Peter Pan because Fidel started turning into a dictator.

"Dictator, huh? Wow, that could never happen in America," he says proudly.

"You never know," I say. But I go on, "My parents are coming to get me out of here soon."

"Then what?" he asks.

"Well, I'm not sure, but probably my father will find a job and we'll find a place to live and I'll go to school, probably a Catholic school . . . stuff like that."

"Uh-huh," he says.

"What about you?" I ask.

"What *about* me?"

"What are you going to do when you get out?" I ask.

He shrugs. "I don't even know *if* I am going to get out. Not until I am eighteen anyway. I guess I can always join the army." He folds the towel with the snot in it. I'm about to tell him to put the towel in the dirty pile bin, but something stops me. Cat Eyes goes on, "So . . . tell me about your life in Cuba."

Suddenly I don't want to say that in Cuba my parents were always around and there wasn't much hitting and that I had a maid make my bed and serve me breakfast. I feel it would be like showing a hungry person some food you couldn't give him. So I say, "My life in Cuba? Well . . . you know . . . it was the usual. School and stuff."

We don't say anything more as we fold the towels. But before I know it, I feel I don't need a pile of towels between us to protect me anymore.

The Look

"Miguel Reyes!" Roll call—Mr. Sherman had just called out my name.

"Present!" I scream. Being in the main dorm meant going through these stupid roll calls. In Florida City, nobody watched us kids; here, they watch all the time.

"Manuel Rivera!"

"Present," mutters Cat Eyes.

Manuel Rivera? I didn't even know Manuel Rivera was Cat Eyes's real name!

"I didn't hear you!" says Mr. Sherman. "Will you please speak up?! Are you asleep or something?"

Cat Eyes's face tenses. He looks at a spot on the floor as if he were drilling a hole into it. Finally, the director moves on.

"Nelson Ayala!" he yells out next.

"Present!" says Nelson.

Then he gets to Julius.

"Julius Johnson!"

"Present," he says softly.

"You are going to be a movie star, right?" says Mr. Sherman sharply.

Julius nods.

"Then say your name like an actor. Let's try again. Julius Johnson," he commands.

"Present!" Julius answers in a nice, clear voice.

Then Mr. Sherman looks down on Julius's night table full of books.

He picks up each one and flips through the pages. "Two of these books are overdue."

"Yes, sir, I'm sorry, I will take them back to the library tomorrow."

"You'd better. There are students who visit the Tottenville library who might really need them."

Julius keeps looking straight ahead.

"Make sure you do! You hear?"

Then the incredible happens. Julius slowly turns his gaze from the wall and looks right into the director's eyes. The look is so strong Mr. Sherman actually takes a step back. "You . . . better . . . er . . . clean up this mess!" he finally says, storming out.

Everyone sighs with relief as soon as Mr. Sherman is gone, and Julius starts to organize his books.

"That director can be mean," says Cat Eyes.

I agree with Cat Eyes, but I saw that the look Julius gave Mr. Sherman definitely bothered him.

Punishment

Today, I am on floor-polishing duty. The droning and spinning of the machine empties my mind and snippets of Cuba fall into the empty spaces: I think of the color of the Caribbean Sea as it crashes against the Malecón roadway now, same as it did before the Revolution and same as it will forever on end, no matter what happens. Then I seem to hear the fruit seller's song, *¡Frutas, naranjas dulces!* And the kid or grandson who helped him—and Ana—poor Ana who never liked me, but whose rebel father died in one of Castro's jails! Then I remember driving around Havana with my grandfather in his old blue Ford or ferrying across Havana Harbor with him. Then again, I remember the funniest thing—the day the bird crapped on Fidel's head, at the rally, and how hard everybody laughed. Damn Fidel!

That last thought makes the machine slip right out of my hands! My yell brings Julius, who was cleaning the bathrooms nearby. We catch it!

"*Gracias*, thank you," I say.

"Sure." He smiles and goes back to work.

But I want to talk more. I want to know about him. My English has gotten much better, and I feel fine using it. Cat Eyes has helped with it though he didn't mean to. He and I always start to talk in Spanish, then fall into a mixture of Spanish and

English, and then before I know it—we are just speaking English! I guess Cat Eyes is kind of a language bridge. Actually, all Puerto Ricans are like a language bridge with all the Spanglish they speak.

"So . . . you want to be an actor?" I ask quickly.

Julius stops and smiles. "Yes, just like Sidney Poitier. When he acts, you really get what he is feeling and thinking."

But then Mr. Sherman busts in on us, shocking all the English words out of me. "Miguel! Julius! What's going on here? Why aren't you polishing the floor?"

I have no idea how to say that *"the machine slipped out of my hands!"*

"And don't tell me you don't understand English," Mr. Sherman says to me. "I caught you two talking!" Then he turns to Julius. "What about you? What are you doing out here, yapping? Can't you do something as simple as clean a bathroom?"

Julius doesn't say anything, but just as he had in the dormitory, he looks Mr. Sherman right in the eye.

"You . . . you," Mr. Sherman almost chokes as he says, "go out into the yard and hold your arms out until I say different!"

"But, sir . . ." I say.

"But, sir, nothing," he practically spits. "In fact—why don't you go join him, Mr. Miguel Reyes!" Sherman marches us outside for our punishment.

If looks could kill, Mr. Sherman would be dead!

Bravery

Outside we stand next to each other, arms outstretched.

"I'm sorry I got you into trouble," I say.

"No problem, he was going to get me anyway."

"So why do you do it?"

"What?"

"Look him in the eye. If you looked down instead of in his eyes, maybe he wouldn't punish you."

"You think that's why he punishes me? Because I look him straight in the eye?"

"Well, yes. It makes him angry that you are not afraid of him."

"You think I'm not afraid of him?"

I twist my head. The sun is going down, and I can barely see him.

"Are you?" I ask.

"What?" he says.

"Afraid of him?"

He answers so quietly I almost can't hear him. "Yes."

"Then why do you look him in the eye?" I ask.

That makes him gulp, throw his head back, look up, and turn his palms to the sky, saying, "Because I have to do *something*! I can't just look down!"

"Okay, okay," I whisper. It has gotten much darker. We cannot really see each other.

"Hey, Julius   " I start, I want to tell him about Cuba, about my stubborn Grandfather Reyes and his blue Ford, about how Ana's father died after fighting for Fidel, about buying oranges from a fruit seller who sang ¡Frutas, naranjas dulces! when I hear a little sniffling, then a little sobbing, then all-out crying.

Julius stops crying after a while. When Mr. Sherman finally calls us in, we throw ourselves on our bunks. The whole room is loud with thinking. Boys are just resting or coughing or looking up at the ceiling. I wonder if Cat Eyes is thinking about his stepfather's butt. Julius has his arms over his face. Maybe he is thinking about being an actor. Or maybe he's wondering why he gets the worst work details and why Mr. Sherman is always on his back.

As I listen to all that's going on, I worry about being a refugee, a person forced to leave their home—and suddenly and crazily, I feel as though I am the luckiest kid here.

Vomit

"Papi, Mami, is something wrong?" I wasn't expecting a call from them. Mr. Sherman looks at me from across his desk.

"Miguel! We're here!" says my father.

I look around the room, thinking they might jump out of a closet, or out from under Mr. Sherman's desk or something. Then I think I didn't hear right. "Wait. What? What did you say?" I ask.

"We are here! In Miami. We received our visas one week ago. We tried to call you from Cuba but couldn't get through fast enough," says my father.

My mother comes on the line. She speaks so fast I can hardly understand her. "We got on the first plane to Miami before the government changed its mind," she says. "The Cuban Refugee Center in Miami found us a place to stay. Catholic Charities is working to fly us to New York to come get you!"

"When . . . ?" I whisper, feeling weak.

"Miguel, let me speak to the director there," says Papi. "We will see you soon . . ."

I hand the phone to Mr. Sherman and try to listen, but thoughts are whirling around in my head. My parents are in the United States—in Miami! They are coming to pick me up here in Staten Island, New York City! My stomach suddenly begins to rumble and then heave. Mr. Sherman hangs up the phone.

"What's the matter? You look green," he says.

I look at him—then throw up all over his desk.

"What the—?

"I'm sorry . . . I don't know what happened," I say, wiping my mouth.

"For heaven's sake," Mr. Sherman groans. "This is ridiculous, Miguel. You and your stomach problems! How could you do such a thing?"

"I don't know," I answer. And I really didn't know. I didn't feel sick. I felt just fine.

"Just clean this up!" he says, tossing paper towels at me and storming out.

I clean up my mess in a daze.

Later, Nelson laughs when I tell him what happened.

"You're nervous about seeing your parents," he says. "Don't worry, Miguel. Maybe they'll be so happy to see you, they'll throw up all over you," he adds, laughing.

Parents

And then they are here.

Nelson, Cat Eyes, Julius, and I are raking leaves when I feel a warm gust of wind. As I turn, I see a taxi coming through the gate, with people inside whose outlines are so familiar my heart leaps. And then I know, it wasn't wind going through me—it was the warmth of my parents' presence going through me! I drop the rake and run toward them so fast I almost fly.

"Whoa," say my friends, calling after me.

"*Hijo,*" says my mother, struggling with the car door to get to me. Her hug almost crushes my bones. "You are so skinny, Miguel. Haven't you been eating?"

My father approaches slowly and extends his hand. I take it—then we crash into each other, hugging. But something is different. Then I know what it is—I am taller than he is.

"My goodness, son, you shot up! I know boys have growth spurts, but you really shot up in seven months!" Then he leans in, whispering, "We did it, son. We got out of Cuba! I had to grease some palms to get our papers, but we did it."

We stumble toward the building. My friends stare.

"These are my friends," I say, finally introducing them, linking them together with my eyes. "Julius, Cat Eyes, and Nelson." My parents are polite to Julius and Cat Eyes and want to know

Nelson's story, but I can tell they want to get going.

"We will talk to Mr. Sherman and begin our journey back to Miami," says Papi finally.

The next day, my parents and I wait for the taxi to arrive. My friends Julius and Cat Eyes and Nelson stand nearby. Too soon, the taxi comes around, grinding to a stop. How do you say good-bye when you feel happy and sad at the same time? As my parents load up, I pull my friends aside.

"Hey, Cat Eyes," I say. "Next time you want to shoot somebody in the butt, look him in the eye instead."

"Huh?" he says.

"Julius will tell you all about it!"

Julius looks at me and smiles.

"And you, Julius—I hope you become a big movie star!"

"You bet, *amigo*."

"See you in Miami," says Nelson.

"You going there?" I ask, surprised.

"You never know," he answers. "*¡Adiós!*"

I remember Cómico. "How many Cubans does it take to say good-bye?" I tease.

Nelson looks at me blankly.

"None," I say. "Because we don't say good-bye. We say *¡Hasta luego!*' See you later!"

Catching Up

I am full of questions on our way to the airport. "Tell me about Grandfather. Does he still drive his blue Ford? Does he talk to it when it doesn't start? Does he still hate to be called a *compañero*? And what about Grizelda? Does she still make you breakfast and run the house?"

"First of all, we couldn't convince your grandfather to come with us." says Mami, then she tries to make a joke. "And yes, I think it was because he didn't want to leave that old blue Ford. And Grizelda went back to her family in the mountains and works in the sugarcane fields when it's harvest time."

"She hates it," adds Papi.

"We can live on money I've saved here in the USA until I find a job," Papi continues. "The Cuban Refugee Center found us a place to stay."

"I picked tomatoes!" I blurt out.

"What!" My mother is shocked.

"For money. When I was at Florida City Camp. We just snuck out . . ."

"You snuck out? Wasn't that dangerous, Miguel?" asks Papi. "Wasn't that breaking some rule?"

"We'll have to talk to Catholic Charities about that," says

Mami to Papi. "Imagine that—letting our boy sneak out to pick tomatoes!"

"It wasn't like that!" I insist.

"Wasn't like what?" says Mami, confused.

"There were Mexicans and Puerto Ricans doing it."

"Mexicans? Puerto Ricans? Picking tomatoes?"

"Yes, to make a living." Suddenly our conversation seems off track, so I tell them about Julius. "He was in foster care a lot."

"Yes, I saw him. I hope he did not scare you!" says Mami, alarmed.

"No, why should he scare me?"

"Well, you just never know . . ."

"We were friends! We talked about being in the same situation."

"What? How could you be in the same situation as an American Black boy in an orphanage?" says Mami. "You're not in foster care. How can you say that?" Mami wails.

"Don't upset your mother, Miguel," says my father. "Being apart has been so hard on all of us."

If telling them about picking tomatoes and Julius upsets them, telling them about Cat Eyes wanting to shoot his step-father in the butt will kill them—so I don't.

"I am so happy we can be together again," says Mami. "We'll be just like we used to be in Cuba."

Can we?

You Don't See Me

It is late when we get to a tiny apartment over a garage in Miami. "Our entranceway in Cuba was bigger than this whole apartment," Mami says wistfully. "You'll have to sleep on the cot next to the sink, Miguel. Is that all right?"

"Sure," I say. "I slept with a bunch of boys practically up my nose at Florida City . . ."

"Go to sleep, *hijo*," says my father, patting me on the head. "We are all tired. We will talk more tomorrow." He starts to light his cigar, then remembers. "I forgot, the owners said they did not want smoking in their house. I'll be right back." And he goes downstairs for his last smoke of the day.

"Well, that'll make us try to get our own house quicker—so your father can smoke indoors!" Then Mami grins at me. "Here, Miguel, let me help you with the sheets," she says.

"I can do it, Mami."

"No, let me help you."

"Really, I can do it," I laugh. "After all, I've slept in two dormitories—actually three dormitories! One in Florida City Camp and two in Mount Loretto, and in all of them I had to make my own bed. I'll never get as good as Grizelda, but . . ." She watches as I tuck in the sheets and fluff up the pillow.

"My goodness," she adds thoughtfully.

I shower, quickly wrap a towel around me, and rush out. "Mami, even in Florida it gets cold sometimes. You know, the United States is so big, you only get to feel how big it is when you travel by train from Miami to New York City. And in Florida City Camp, they wanted us to eat slimy green vegetables called okra! Yuck!"

"What happened to your robe?" Mami asks.

"What?"

"The robe I bought you with the cowboys on it."

I am surprised that I had actually forgotten about the robe. "I . . . er . . . I guess I lost it in one of the moves."

She sighs sadly. "Lost it. It was so nice. One of the last nice things I bought you." She turns away, sniffling.

I rush to her side and stub my toe. One of Cómico's favorite curses slips out of my mouth.

"¡Muchacho!" she says, shocked. "Where did you ever hear such language?" she scolds.

My curse hangs in the air like a fart. My father returns and smells trouble right away. "What's wrong?" he asks.

Mami tearfully answers. "Do you know what word your son just used?" She whispers it in his ear.

"No," he says weakly.

"Mami, I'm sorry, but I heard words worse than that here in the United States."

"I wonder what other bad habits he's picked up here," says Mami to Papi, as if I wasn't in the room. As if I was the little kid my parents sent here months ago.

Reunited

"How many Cubans does it takes to mow a lawn?"

I wake up, thinking I must've been dreaming about Cómico. Ha! But it was just the buzzing sounds of a lawn mower. I roll over knowing Mami is shopping for food and Papi is looking for a job. But just when I am at the edge of sleep and ready to fall in, I hear it again, loud and clear. "Come on, Papi. Guess how many Cubans it takes to mow a lawn." This was no dream. This *is* no dream! I look out the window. It's Cómico! I throw on some clothes and go outside!

"Cómico, it's you!"

Cómico's mouth falls open. He is just as shocked as I am! "Wha . . . wha . . ."

"Wha . . . wha . . . yourself!" I laugh.

"Miguel! What are you doing here?"

"I live here! With my mother and father! They came. What about you?"

"Mowing this lawn with *my* father! I mean, I live here in Miami too!"

"*¿Quién es?*" says Cómico's father, joining us. He has the same red hair as his son.

"This is the guy I picked tomatoes with at Florida City Camp. Remember I told you, Papi?"

"Pleased to meet you," says Cómico's father.

Cómico tells me they are waiting for his mother to get her travel documents, but now his father is here, and they are trying to get a lawn-mowing business going. Then he teases, "Hey, your stomach is not rolling over your belt anymore and you got some hairs growing on your lip!" I ask about Osvaldo.

"He got sent to Denver—but don't worry, once his parents get to the USA, he'll come to Miami. We all seem to be settling in Miami because it's so close to Cuba we share the same bit of sky . . . I don't know . . . anyway, we're here!"

Then he turns to his father. "Osvaldo was the other kid we worked picking tomatoes with, remember!"

"You guys were sure industrious." He smiles, then says, "So, let me ask *you*. How many Cubans *does* it take to mow a lawn?"

"Aww, Pops," says Cómico. "Don't tell my jokes. You don't tell them as good as me!"

His father ignores him and goes on, "Two, it takes two. You and your friend Miguel here."

"Good one, Papi. Good one," says Cómico.

"I *can* help," I say, excited about the idea.

"Good! You two take over!" And his father sits on the steps and smokes a little cigar.

Cómico shows me what to do. We mow and talk and talk and mow. He tells me that Primero never came back, I tell him about my fake appendicitis attack.

When we are done, Cómico says, "You want a job with us?"

"Me? You think I can work with you guys?" I say.

"Yeah, before school starts. We'll make some money. It'll be just like when we were picking tomatoes. I'll convince my father . . ." he says.

"Okay," I say. "We'll do it."

Adjusting

"No! No, child of mine is going to mow lawns!" Mami screams the minute I tell her my idea. She adjusts the plastic bag on her head that keeps the black hair dye from dripping onto her face.

"But, Mami, I see kids mowing lawns all over the place. It's the American thing to do!"

"What if you pinch a finger?" she says, catching a black drip with a tissue.

"Mami, I handled a big floor polisher at Mount Loretto, and other large machines too."

"My poor baby," she says, hugging me and almost getting dye on my face.

"Mami, please—I am not a baby! Look, I have hair growing over my lip."

She steps back, then stares, examining my face. "I *do* see some hairs," she exclaims. Then quickly, "Shave it! No hair on your face like Fidel and all those other crazy hairy rebels!"

My father comes home. Mami and I stop our skirmish and look at him expectantly.

"Only jobs cleaning toilets or washing dishes," he sighs. "We have to make our money last a little longer."

"I know, *mi amor*, that's why I am dyeing my own hair. To save money."

MIGUEL

"I can make money," I say, telling him about the mowing.

When I am done, Papi looks at the bag on Mami's head. "I'll let your mother decide," he says, throwing up his hands.

I look to Mami.

"No," she says, her eyes hard on me.

Seeds

Cómico and his father mow over a patch of grass outside our house when Mami comes running out. "You are not mowing lawns, are you?" she scolds me.

"No," I say. "But this is Cómico—"

Suddenly she snaps her head. "What's that fragrance?"

"This plant we just mowed over," says Cómico.

My mother drops to her knees. "Oh yes," she says, suddenly enchanted. "I love that fragrance."

Cómico's father joins us. *"¿Señora . . . ?"*

"Oh . . ."

We introduce them.

"I'm so sorry," says Mami, getting up. "I forgot my manners. Nice to meet you both, it's just that the plant, the fragrance, the—well, it just reminds me of Cuba!"

"Seguro que sí," says Cómico's father. "It's a wonderful ground cover. There is a similar variety in Cuba. It is very strong and beautiful."

"Sí," says Mami enthusiastically. "First there is a waxy green leaf, then a bunch of tiny yellow flowers. That is when it is the most fragrant."

"And then," adds Cómico's father, "the flowers die and the seeds are blown all over."

"Where they land and grow, bringing beauty everywhere," Mami finishes. "How could I have not noticed them before?" she says.

"You are just getting used to being here in the United States, *señora*," Cómico's father says quietly. "When your eyes get adjusted to being in America, you will see more beautiful things."

My mother smiles. "I guess you are right." She turns to me and sighs. "Miguel . . ."

I lean in.

"Bring your friends in for a *limonada* drink after you help them mow the lawn." Then she looks me in the eye. "And I'll buy you a thermos so you can take a cool drink wherever you work with them."

I catch my breath and think I am hearing things. "Wait—did you say you'd buy me a thermos? To take to work?" I ask, hoping I heard right.

"*Sí.*"

"Does this mean I can work with Cómico and his father?" I almost can't believe it.

She shrugs. "Of course. We are all Cubans." Then she turns abruptly and goes back inside.

I try to make a joke. "How many fragrant plants does it take to pull Cubans together?"

Cómico looks at me, and we say at the same time, "One. Just one!"

Park

My parents and I sit in a plaza in our neighborhood full of Cubans, relaxing in our new world. The sound of dominos slapping tables fills the air like conga music.

Ta! Ta! Ta! Ta! Ta!

The men, laughing when they win, or complaining when they lose, create another familiar sound from Cuba. Groups of other men talk of Fidel Castro and gesture so hard they create a breeze that moves the sweet smell of *cafecito* from a coffee shop nearby all over.

"I almost feel like I am in Cuba," says Papi. "You remember how in Cuba, the plaza would be full of people taking in the night air?"

"*Sí,*" says Mami. "Remember the sea spray coming over the Malecón as we drove along it? I wonder if your father, Don Reyes, is still driving that blue Ford up and down that roadway."

"I bet he is. My father is a stubborn man," says Papi. "But it wasn't really the car he didn't want to leave. It was Cuba."

We sit with that and listen to the world around us. "We couldn't bring much from Cuba, but we sure brought our style!" Mami adds.

"You got that right, Mami," I say, eyeing her hair, which looks like a nest of *croquetas* on her head.

Then Papi says, "You know, I have a thought—what do you

think of me getting a real estate license and opening up my own office?"

"That's a wonderful idea," says Mami, looking around. "I have a feeling this will be a growing community."

"If we work hard . . ." says Papi.

"We can help it grow," says Mami.

"Just like those plants," I say.

"What?" says Mami.

"Just like those plants you and Cómico's father were talking about."

"Ah yes . . ." she says. "I see more and more of them every day! All I had to do was look."

We smile at each other and let the sounds in the park sweep over us.

Then she teases, "When did your feet get so big!"

"When you weren't looking," I answer.

We laugh.

I look around at all the little Cuban stores squeezing to get through on the street.

Lo Tengo Cigar Shop squeezing out from between Friedman's Bakery and Finding Underthings, the lingerie store.

The Caribe Music Store reaching out from between Goldblatt's Meats and Stoutmen's Shirt Shop.

La Maravilla Coffee Place sandwiched between two other old Miami shops.

These Cuban shops are like the strong little yellow plants, *fuerte* enough to fight their way through bricks and cement, growing toward the light of the sun.

People can only be free if they are truly educated.
—JOSÉ MARTÍ

ZULEMA

CUBAN COUNTRYSIDE · 1961

"Zulema! Have you gotten the water?"

Quickly, I put the book of fairy tales aside and think of Ana in Havana. She gave me the book on my visit to Havana two years ago—and I still can't help laughing when I remember how the dove pooped on Fidel's head that day at the rally!

"Zulema!"

Quickly I peek through the cracks in the walls at my mother.

Did she hear me laughing instead of working? No—she is too busy working herself, pounding the corn.

Poom, poom, poom!

"I am going *now!*" I say, grabbing the clay jug. The sun burns my eyes the second I step out the door, so I look away, trying to ignore it on my way to the well. *Imposible.*

Before filling the clay jugs, I take a sip of water and pat my eyes cool with my wet hands. The water is light and refreshing. Not as it will be when I fill my jug. Then it will become crushing and heavy as stone. As I fill the jug and carry the water inside, my muscles tremble like taut ropes.

"Zulema, have you swept the floor?" I put the jug down and grab the broom, shooing the chicken off the table and moving into the doorway so Mamá can see me. But my mother doesn't stop her pounding or even look my way. She just pounds and pounds and pounds. *Poom, poom, poom!* I sweep our dirt floor, making sure the dirt stays packed down.

"Zulema—please bring me water!" I take a deep breath as I pour some water into a jar and take it to her. The sweat runs down the middle of her back, and I see she is even more soaked than I am. When she returns the jar, she pats my cheek. The sweat from her hand blends with the sweat on my face, and I pull away. I don't want to be like her when I grow up. I want to have all my teeth when I am her age. This idea makes me embarrassed for my feelings. I look away.

"Go on with your chores," she says with a smile.

I am relieved to get away and feed the chickens, and the pigs I have named Sabroso and Chichón, who grunt and move, covering me in a cloud of their stink. The sweat from my brow drips into my eyes and stings. I dry them with my dress. The fabric scratches my eyes.

"Zulema!" Mamá calls out to me again. "What are you doing?" Why does she ask me what I am doing? What does she think I'm doing? I am doing what I do every day. Get water, sweep the floor, feed the chickens, be covered in a cloud of stink from the pigs. What else is there to do?

"Are you daydreaming again when your father is out working in the fields and waiting for his water?" I pour water into my father's jug, and I'm off.

Water

I carry the water down the winding path and into a row of plantain trees that are just a bit taller than me. The long bananas grow toward the sky, forcing me to reach up to get them when they ripen. I like doing that better than digging into the ground to get yuca. Digging makes me feel like our pigs Sabroso and Chichón, rooting for food. Finally I hear Papá's oxen. The oxen are too dumb to be given names because all they do is work, like my father.

"Where have you been?" he says sharply, taking off his hat and wiping his brow with his kerchief. He reaches for the jug of water with his big puffy hands, then drinks. His Adam's apple slides up and down as he gulps.

"Go," he says when he is done, pushing the almost-empty jug into my hand. He groans, stretching his back before returning to work.

Taking the long way home, I wonder about the trees and the clouds and the bugs that fly all around. The day is clear until suddenly the air cools and changes direction. In the distance, I see rain pouring from a dark cloud moving toward my house. Who will get to my house first, the rain or me? I decide to race it. But first I drink the last bit of water in the jug that will weigh nothing as water flows through my arms and legs.

ZULEMA

As I run, the newly cooled air fills my lungs and I forget everything. Before I know it, I am in front of my house waiting for the slowpoke rain to catch up. My mother is at the clothesline.

"Don't just stand there," scolds Mamá. "Help me take these clothes off the line before the rain gets here! I don't want your dress to get wet. It might not dry in time to go to town tomorrow."

"We're going to town tomorrow?" I ask.

"Yes," she says. "There's a community meeting."

I am so happy I feel light as water when it becomes vapor.

Meeting

My father is the last to sign in. He presses his thumb into the ink, then onto the paper along with everyone else's thumbprints, to prove he is here.

"The meeting will come to order," community leader for the Defense of the Revolution, *el compañero* Linares, announces.

I skip up and down the aisle, trying to see everything Jacinto sells at once—cans with pictures of olives or tomatoes on them. White sneakers tossed in a basket, ruffled dresses in lemon and lime colors that float like wearable clouds above my head. Against the wall I see bottles of rum with gold designs on the labels. Next to them are bottles of black beer labeled with crowns. On the walls are calendars with pictures of pirates and Gypsies for each month.

I pick out a magazine from the rack. Turning the pages quietly, I look at the photo of a woman with a bit of cream on her finger. I can tell from her carefree face that it is beauty cream, but there must be more about it. Is it to keep you beautiful? Or to keep you moist? Does the ad tell me how it smells? Not understanding the words sprinkled around her face makes me feel as if I am looking through fog at something just out of reach. Or like how on some mornings, the haze is so thick I barely see my mother pounding corn, and only know she is there because of the sound. I look at the picture this way and that, and touch the magazine as if that will make me understand it better . . .

"You better put that back!" It's Cecilia sneaking up and looking at me with such lizard eyes I think that her tongue will sneak out and catch a fly any minute. "You're not supposed to touch anything if you are not going to buy it," she adds. Cecilia is my age but always tries to act older.

"Shut up, will you!" I warn.

"I won't—you're not supposed to touch anything unless you're going to pay for it."

I am just about to push her away when I hear, "Zulema!"

It's my cousin, Nilo! I am so happy to hear his voice, I put the magazine back and go outside.

Nilo

"Is Cecilia here?" Nilo asks.

"Yes," I say, annoyed he asked about her before even saying hello to me. But his grin is so open, I fall into his smile. "Hello, cousin." I grin back.

He slips off the horse he is sharing with his mother, Tía Lita. On another horse coming up behind is his father, my tío Zenón, saying, "We're late." He pats me on the head.

Nilo takes the reins, ties the horses, and then we run inside just in time to hear my father say, "Fidel has gone too far!" Beating the Yankees in the Bay of Pigs fiasco has gone to his head. Now he thinks he can do anything.

Tío Zenón signs in with his thumbprint as Nilo and I go to the back of the store. People argue back and forth about how far Castro has gone.

Nilo puts a finger to his lips, bidding me to be quiet. When the arguing about Fidel is at its loudest, Nilo quietly opens a big jar of candy from the United States and offers me a handful of the waxy orange sweets. All at once, Cecilia appears out of nowhere. "I saw you take that," she says, her lizard eyes turning into slits. "I'm telling . . ."

"But, Cecilia," whispers Nilo, grinning quickly. "I stole them for you."

"What?" she says.

"For you," Nilo says, smiling at her all syrupy. Then he gives her the rest of the candy. "I stole the candy for you. You won't tell on me now, will you?"

Cecilia thinks, then holds out her hand.

"It is my pleasure to give you my candy," Nilo says formally. Cecilia stuffs the candy in her mouth as I hear my father's voice above all the rest. "This is terrible. Ridiculous. An imposition!" he spits. "An army of teachers? Why does the army have to do everything? Ever since Fidel's forces beat back the Americans at the Bay of Pigs, he thinks the army can do anything—think for us, dream for us, make us dinner. Can the army do that, too!"

"Santiago, please," says my mother.

"This is a crazy idea," he hisses.

I watch Cecilia chew until I see the orangey-white waxy stuff gather in the corners of her mouth.

"That's disgusting," I whisper.

"So?" she says defiantly. "I like it!"

"Let her eat it," says Nilo, defending her.

Disgusted by both of them, I go back and sneak the magazine off the rack. Suddenly, out of the corner of my eye I see Cecilia throw up! Nilo takes off his neckerchief and helps wipe her face.

"What's going on back there?" says Linares.

"Nothing!" says Nilo. "We'll clean it up."

Cecilia's parents, Chismosa and Viejo, rush to her side.

"Are you sick?" asks her mother.

Sick of eating, I think to myself, turning away from them

and looking at the magazine as *el compañero* Linares continues. "Students will come into your homes to teach you to read!"

I almost drop the magazine. Did I hear right? Did *el compañero* Linares just say students will come into our house to teach us to read?

"And sneer at us with their high-class ways!" says my father. "Never. Let's go! Zulema! Now!"

I put the magazine back and follow my mother and father outside. My father gets the *carreta*; his anger makes the horses skittish. As he settles them, Nilo rushes up to me. "Here," he says quickly.

"What . . . ?"

"Shhh . . . a prize for you instead of candy . . ."

And Nilo pushes the magazine I was looking at into my hand.

"Nilo," I say, surprised.

He winks at me. "See you next time."

I shove the magazine under my dress.

As the *carreta*'s wheels turn, I listen to my parents argue. "I will not allow students to sleep in my house. No!"

"Stop arguing with the authorities. You are going to get us into trouble," says Mama.

"What authorities? Linares? Bah," Papa sneers. "He's just a poor farmer like the rest of us."

"He was a poor farmer like the rest of us—now he's a CDR man watching us, making sure we do whatever Fidel says—and at this moment Fidel says learn to read."

Papá explodes. "No. I don't want high-class, little *habaneros* strangers, who can spy on us or denounce for any reason we don't even know about, living in my house and thinking they are better than me! No!"

I feel the magazine, almost hot against my thigh, all the way home.

Brigadistas

A week later, I see two soldiers in the distance coming to arrest me, I'm sure, for having the magazine Nilo stole for me.

Running inside, I climb up on the bed and hide it between the wall and the thatched roof. Then I go out and wait with my mother, my heart in my mouth.

Mamá turns to me from grinding corn. "Soldiers," she says. "I thought the Revolution was over," and she goes back to pounding.

But I'm relieved they are not soldiers, but a girl, a little older than me, and a young man, wearing what look like military uniforms. But not quite. They dismount and approach us, smiling.

"My name is Carlos," says the boy. "And this is Carmen," he says, introducing the girl as he helps her dismount. "We are *Los brigadistas*, come to teach!"

Carmen reminds me of someone. Was it the girl in the magazine with the cream on her finger and curly black hair and eyebrows that each arch up in the middle? All at once, it comes to me!

"We represent the Campaña Nacional de Alfabetización en Cuba," says Carmen. "We are staying over at Don Jacinto's store in the village until we pick a house to have the reading lessons in."

She's one of the girls I met with Ana in Havana two years ago at the rally!

"May we go inside?" says Carlos.

"Of course, but just the girl," says Mamá. "No man in the house without my husband." He holds the horses as Carmen turns toward the house. I pull my mother back and tell her how we met Carmen at the rally.

Mamá looks confused. "You mean when the bird pooped on Fidel's head!"

"Yes!"

Recognition sweeps over her face. We catch up to Carmen. "Wait!" I say moments before she enters the house. "Don't you remember me?"

She looks at me blankly.

"At the rally! In Havana! We stayed with Ana!"

Carmen sucks in her breath. "Oh my goodness! Yes! Ana!" Her face becomes dark. "She was my friend. We went to school together."

"What happened to Ana and her family?" asks Mamá.

"They abandoned the Revolution after her father went to jail and died of a heart attack. Ana wrote me a letter saying they were leaving Cuba," she says flatly.

We are silent for a moment, each careful not to give an opinion about the Revolution. I remember you never know when you can be denounced.

"Do you remember the bird pooping on Fidel's head?" I say.

"Oh yes," she giggles. Thank goodness every Cuban finds that funny. It opens a way for us. We go into the house, laughing.

Uncertainty

Carmen eyes the chicken on the table.

"Have a seat!" I offer.

"*¿Café?*" offers Mamá.

"No, *gracias*," says Carmen, looking around but focusing on the floor. "Is that a dirt floor?" she says, digging her toe in it. "Oh my goodness, it's just like Ana's father said it was!"

"Speaking of Ana, I want to show you the book she gave me." I run to get it, and when I come back, Carmen is still examining the floor.

She looks up. "What is your name again?" she asks.

"Zulema," I say. "Look—this is the book Ana gave me. Will you teach me to read it?"

Carmen frowns at it. "Nice book of fairy tales, but we have other books to learn from first! Ones that have important information about the Revolution in them. Books that will help you understand Fidel's great cause!"

I keep my disappointment hidden. I wanted to read fairy tales. Later, outside, Carlos is excited about the coincidence. "This proves this was meant to be," he says. "Your house is perfect for community literacy lessons."

"Everybody will come here to learn?" asks Mamá.

"Yes, we will be back in a few days," they say, riding away.

ZULEMA

The minute they are gone, I run back to the house to look at the book Ana gave me and run my fingers over the words. When I go to the bathroom to do my business, I notice the words on the newspapers that line the walls. Then I get the magazine Nilo stole for me back from under the roof and look at that. Before I know it—I feel eyes boring into my back.

"Where did you get that magazine?" It's Mamá.

I'm caught. She waits. "Nilo saved it for me . . ." I say slowly.

She raises her arm and for a moment I think she is going to hit me, but she doesn't. She scratches the top of her head instead, saying, "Don't let your father see it."

Suddenly I know we are on the same side, so I ask, "Do you think he'll let the *brigadistas* teach here?"

She shrugs. "Get some water."

I get the water. My hope floats.

Sereno

Papá comes home, and I run out and give him a jar of water even before he gets off the oxcart. He looks angrier than usual and brings his quiet rage to dinner. Mamá presents him with a plate of food. Then she waits until he's taken a spoonful before she tells him all that went on. With a mouth full of food, he can't answer as quickly.

"Ugh." He tries but can't get the words out. "*Agua,*" he commands. He is done swallowing when he says, "I told you, no teachers in this house!"

I drop his jar onto the soft ground. Papá explodes. "What is wrong with you! How could you drop the jar?" My mouth opens, but no words come out. The jar is not broken. Not even cracked.

He finishes his dinner, grunts, and goes outside to sit on a rocking chair on the porch and smoke his cigar. Mamá and I tiptoe around, cleaning the plates and putting the kitchen back in order. Cricket song announces the night, so I light the lanterns.

"*Agua,*" my father barks from outside.

I get a jar of water and take it out to him.

The light from his cigar joins the light from my lantern.

As I wait for him to drink, Mamá warns from inside, "You

two are going to get sick from *el sereno* in the air if you stay out there."

"That is an old superstition," he says. "There is no *sereno* in the air. It is 1961, not 1861!"

"That's right—it is 1961—time to learn to read and write!" Mamá replies sharply.

Papá grunts again and sucks on his cigar. "I am the man of this house," he calls to her. "What I say goes! No one learns anything until I say so!" Then after a moment, "Bedtime! Now!"

He pulls the cigar out of this mouth with his fat fingers as if he is looking for a fight—he soon gets one.

Rounds One, Two, and Three

Carlos and Carmen come back so early one day, Papá has not even harnessed the oxen to the cart. I throw on my dress and fuss around as though I am preparing to get water, but I am really listening as I get a jug.

"Sir," says Carlos. "Your wife has probably told you that we have decided that your house is the best one in which to hold community literacy classes."

"I don't care what my wife said, or what you think you've decided. There will be no *brigadistas* in my house," says Papá, leading the oxen.

"But Fidel has promised to make Cuba one hundred percent literate within a year."

My father starts to say something—but then thinks better of it.

"But I think I met your daughter when you went to Havana for the celebration rally!" adds Carmen happily. "What a coincidence!"

"Yes, remember, Papá?" I say, offering him the last sip of water from the jug before I go to refill it.

"So what?" he says. "Go fill that jug!"

"*Compañero*, wouldn't you like to be able to sign your name?" asks Carlos.

My father twitches at being called *compañero*, but he goes on, "No, my thumbprint is enough. Besides, you will be interfering with my work."

"No, we would only teach when you are not working," says Carlos quickly. "We would stop whenever there is work to do."

"There is always work to do," barks my father.

"We'd help you," says Carmen. "We want to get a real taste of the life of a farmer. Fidel says city people should understand how you people live."

I come back and offer water. "Would anybody like some water . . . ?"

My father glares as he drinks.

"Zulema, wouldn't you like to read and write?" Carmen asks me.

My father answers for me. "No! Zulema will be too busy working."

"Like we said, we'll help her!" says Carmen.

"What do you kids know about working on a farm?" says Papá finally.

"We would learn!" says Carmen. "That's what Fidel says all along. Country people and city people will learn from one another!"

Carlos and Carmen follow Papá around like little puppies as he puts the rest of his tools into the back of the wagon. They even run alongside him as he drives the oxen out into the fields.

"Get away, you'll get hurt," Papá says gruffly, urging the oxen to go faster.

Carlos and Carmen watch him drive away.

"We will keep trying, *compañera!*" Carlos calls out to Mamá and me as they get on their horses and ride away in the opposite direction.

"Will Papá let them teach here?" I ask Mamá when I see the last of them.

She sighs, saying, "I don't know."

Round two. The next time Carmen and Carlos come, it's so early it's still dark outside.

"Hello!" Carlos calls out. "Here, we are ready to help!"

"Me too," adds Carmen.

Papá bolts out of bed. "Those kids are a bother," he says to Mamá as she puts on her dress.

"Give them a chance," says Mamá, heading to make *café* in the *fogón.*

"Nobody gets a chance until I say so," barks my father.

Mamá knows when to keep quiet. Papá goes out to speak to the *brigadistas* as I peek from the door. All I see is my father shaking his head no as Carmen and Carlos nod their heads yes.

On the third day, it rains. As I watch it gather on the roof and find its way down in rivulets like ribbons, I see Carmen and Carlos approach, slipping and sliding in the mud. My father ignores them and leaves for the fields as they stand drenched and stranded. I invite them onto the porch and give them rags to dry with. "Come back tomorrow," I whisper.

When it clears a bit, I take my father water. The fields are muddy and soft. Papá is frustrated because though it is easy to plow soft earth, seeds don't stay where he puts them. Suddenly his plow hits a big rock. The handle seems to come alive, jumping back and hitting him in the face!

"Agh!" he roars, looking up, blaming the sky, cursing the world! He looks at me and I see painful tears welling up, and he says, "What? Do you really want these *brigadistas* coming around?"

I am scared but give the tiniest nod yes as I hand him the water. He drinks, then presses the cool clay jug against his cheek before handing it back to me. "Go!" he says. As I turn away, I hear him softly ask the heavens, "What am I supposed to do?!"

Two days later, Carmen moves in.

Chamber Pot

Carmen unpacks. I have the book of fairy tales Ana gave me in my hand, but I am distracted by Carmen's underwear. Piles of pretty pink slips and undershirts the same color as her pink nails. Her sleep shirt is flouncy. Her pile of socks is creamy white.

"I am so glad you are excited about reading," she says, noticing my book. "But we have to do things in order. First, we have to get used to each other. Fidel says *guajiros* must get to know city people, and city people must get to know *guajiros*. That's why he had all you people go to Havana! Remember when you stayed with Ana's family? And we met at the rally?"

"Yes, of course," I answer, "but . . ." Carmen is too excited to really listen.

"Now, let me set up! This is what the government has given us: a hammock, notebooks, pencils, and, of course, kerosene-powered lanterns. Our lanterns and your lanterns will give us a *luz brillante*—a brilliant light. We will bring a brilliant light to you people."

When Papá comes home, I run out with a jar of water for him, and to see what his mood is, but Carmen brushes past me. "*¡Buenos días, compañero!* I was just getting ready to help serve dinner."

Papá rolls his eyes and goes to the well to wash up. Mamá

insists Carmen just sit with us this first night. Mamá serves Papá, then Carmen, then me. "Please, *compañera*, next time I will serve myself," says Carmen, staring at her plate of yuca and rice. "We have yuca in Havana," she says, taking a tiny little bite.

I wonder how she will ever finish dinner taking such small bites.

"Fidel Castro says education is a two-way street," she giggles. "As you learn from me, I will learn from you!"

My father yawns and finishes his dinner in three noisy gulps. Carmen decides to clear the plates. "Where's the garbage?" she asks, looking around.

"We don't throw food away here," I say.

"Like you people do in Havana!" adds Papá savagely. "We work hard for our food. If we don't eat it, the pigs will get the leftovers."

"I'm sorry, I just thought they were leftovers to get thrown away. In Havana, we would throw this out."

"Well, guess what—this isn't Havana, is it?" says Papá. Then he goes outside to have his evening cigar.

Carmen carefully sets her hammock up over the kitchen table. The air is so tense I am relieved when Papá announces bedtime and goes to bed.

"Good-night, Carmen," says Mamá.

"*Sí*, good-night," says Carmen. She turns away and carefully puts her sleep shirt on, then takes her clothes off from underneath. She falls asleep almost the minute her head hits the hammock.

Mamá whispers to me, "We forgot the chamber pot!"

"Ah yes!" I get the extra chamber pot from the cabinet and set it where Carmen is sure to see it if she has to go do her business in the middle of the night. Long after, I hear my parents snoring and I have fallen asleep myself, I hear a scream. We all three run to the front room. Carmen's hammock is empty. We hear another scream. Rushing out, we see Carmen running out of the outhouse. Her boots are undone, she holds up her pants with one hand and a lantern with her other. "Something bit me," she says breathlessly.

Papá takes the lantern from her and goes into the outhouse. "There is nothing in there to bite you," he says wearily. "I told you this was not going to work," he whispers to Mamá, whisking by her.

Inside, I point to the chamber pot. "You don't have to get dressed to go to the outhouse at night," I say to Carmen. "You can just pee in the pot."

Her eyes get wide. "There? I'm supposed to do my business there?!"

How can she teach me to read when she doesn't even know where to pee?

She does everything else wrong too. Sweeps the floor so hard she disturbs the packed dirt. Gets more chicken feed on herself than on the chickens. The pigs in the corner make her gag. Even filling the water jugs is too hard, and she ends up tipping one over before we are done.

But still—in the night when she tests her lamps and our lanterns, there is light.

Brilliant Light

I close the outhouse door behind me and stare at our home. No longer is it a poor, thatched-roof *guajiro* house with openings all over that let weather in—it is *brillante* in the night, like a house full of shooting stars. But it is not full of real stars—it is full of kerosene lamps shining with purpose and *brigadista* brilliance. I wonder if that's what ideas look like, and if ideas are even brighter than stars.

"Wasting kerosene—that's all that's going on here!" my father grumbles as I come near.

Eladia and Diego and their two-year-old baby twins arrive carrying chairs to sit on. Carmen flits around greeting everyone nervously. I have the book Ana gave me and offer it to Carmen when she is near.

"Yes, of course," she says. "But I told you, I have other books . . ."

Nilo rides up, interrupting. "Is Cecilia here?" he asks, getting off his horse.

"No, not yet."

"Stop playing around, you two!" my father scolds from the porch.

Nilo and I look at each other and shrug. My father is

being grouchier than ever tonight. More people come. The newly married couple María and Luis arrive holding hands. Chismosa and her old husband, Viejo, arrive with lizard-eyed Cecilia.

"Let me help you with your chair," says Nilo to Cecilia the minute he sees her. "I'll sit next to you."

"I hope the house doesn't fall down with all these people in it," grumps my father.

We go inside. Carmen has taken her hammock down, and I push the chicken off the table to make way for my father so he can sit at the head of the table and feel special, but instead he sits as far away from everyone as possible.

"Good evening, everyone," says Carmen. "I am so happy to see you all and excited to begin our reading journey! Please take your seats."

I sit with the book Ana gave me, in case Carmen wants to use it . . .

"*Now*, we must learn to read from the special revolutionary books the government has assigned us!" Carmen shows everyone a picture in her book. "The first thing we will do is discuss this picture," she says.

"Wait a minute," my father grumbles. "How is looking at a picture going to help us read?"

"We begin to read by looking at pictures and talking about the Revolution!" she says with excitement.

"I knew this reading stuff was just propaganda! I tell you. I am sick of it *already*!" Papá says.

People scrape around in their chairs, muttering, "Let's get started." "Give her a chance." "For heaven's sake."

"What's there to say about that picture?" says Papá, as if the very sight of it makes him mad. "Except that it's a picture of a farmer, a man in a suit, some oxen, and a soldier."

I'm getting so angry at him for interrupting, I think I may spit in his water tomorrow!

"Yes, but what are they *to each other*?" Carmen goes on. "You see, the farmer represents you people—the man in the suit is capitalism—standing between you and your oxen—and the soldier represents militarism and how this is a war on illiteracy . . ."

My father groans.

"Now," says Carmen, "let's begin the conversation."

There is silence. Papa groans again.

"Come on," urges Carmen. "Anything you say is valid."

Papá glares as the conversations begin.

Viejo begins carefully. "I had an ox that looked just like that one!"

"Is that man in the suit supposed to be President Kennedy? He has a lot of hair . . ." says Chismosa.

Eladia and Diego talk about how hard it is to make enough money to feed their kids.

Mama talks about how nice it was for Fidel to send us a picture.

Suddenly we hear snoring, then a crash behind me. Everyone turns. My father has fallen asleep and slipped off his chair.

Everybody laughs. My father stands up quickly. I can see

his face turning red from his neck up like a wave of nausea when you've eaten something bad. The redness seems to travel through his ears and hair and end up at the top of his head, where his rage bursts into beads of sweat that travel down his face.

"I'm a working man. I'm tired," he says, defending himself.

My mother stands. *"¿Quieres café?"* She offers him coffee, but I know she is covering, protecting him, the way she does me.

Nilo and Cecilia keep snickering.

I kick Nilo's chair, hard. He falls over. Then I kick Cecilia's chair so she falls over too. That shuts them up!

Brokeback Fields

I wake Carmen up before the rooster crows.

"Whaaat . . . ?"

"Try to help my father in the fields today," I whisper.

"Huh . . ."

"Even if you fail, he'll know you tried."

After a moment, she agrees.

"I'm ready to go out into the fields with you," she says to Papá the minute he's had his coffee.

Mamá answers for him. "What? No! Stay here! Farming is man's labor. Too hard for you."

I glance at Carmen but busy myself with the water jars.

"Nope! Last night *el compañero* Soto said he was tired and had lots of work to do. I want to help."

"All right," says Papá slowly. "Sometimes a nail does not believe in the hammer until it is hit."

"What does that mean?" asks Carmen. "Is that a country folk saying?"

"Come," says Papá. "You'll know soon enough."

I pull Carmen aside and give her an old straw hat. "Take this—wear it at all times or the sun will make your hair hot to the touch, even before it burns a hole in your head—and work slowly, like the oxen."

I think about Carmen as I do my chores and rush midday so I can take them some water.

Carmen is drenched with sweat, her face red and wild with effort. She gulps the water down hard. Her pink nails are torn and ragged.

Papá drinks his share, and then he offers, "Ready to go back to the house, Carmen?"

"No, no, I can work the whole day." She is embarrassed, but I see angry tears as well. When Carmen comes back home at the end of the day, I can tell she is almost as broken as her beautiful pink nails are. Her palms raw.

"I am okay," she says, even as she slumps onto the porch, her head leaning against the column. "I'll get used to this hard work."

But I can tell that she is in pain. She becomes a puzzle I am curious to solve. "Why do you do it?" I ask her when Mamá busies herself cooking, and Papá is washing up.

"Do what?" she asks.

"Come out here to teach us when you have to work so hard."

She sits up as if a thunderbolt shot through her. Forgetting the blisters forming on her fingers, the sunburn on her forehead, the ache I imagine blossoming in her back—she answers:

"To do something different! To have a life different from what my parents planned out for me, of getting married and having children and living in the same neighborhood in Havana so I could be near them, and going to church every Sunday. UGH!"

"What's wrong with doing those things?" I ask quietly.

"Nothing! But I wanted to make sure that I *wanted* to do them—that I wasn't just doing them because I was supposed to!

ZULEMA

I didn't want to go from being somebody's daughter to somebody's wife without even thinking about it! I just wanted to try something new, for me. I wanted to see what I could do for myself—by myself!" She stops, then looks at me closely. "Is that so terrible?"

I see hot tears coming out from her eyes.

Papá walks by and makes believe he doesn't see, but I know he does.

"P" Is for Papá and Pencil

The letters are not silent. The letters make sounds called vowels. I am learning.

"*A, e, i, o,* and *u!*" says Carmen, writing them on the sheet of tin used as a blackboard. "Copy what I write as you repeat after me." She writes a letter and makes the sound, and we repeat, until our lesson sounds like a song.

Carmen goes on with all the rest of the letters and sounds. They dance around my head even as I write them down.

Nilo sneaks over and shows me his notebook. He has drawn a round face with big ears and crazy hair. "Hey, Zulema, look! It's you!" he says, laughing.

"Shhh," I say, not wanting to be distracted. "Write the letters! Look—even Cecilia is writing."

Nilo's eyes light up. "I'll go see what she is doing!" and he goes over to her.

Carmen walks around and looks over everyone's shoulder. She stops at Papá. "*Compañero* Soto," she says. "You are holding the pencil incorrectly." Papá holds the pencil as if it were a machete. Carmen shows Papá how to hold the pencil by trying to separate his thick fingers.

He tries. "Like this?" he asks.

"*Sí*," says Carmen helpfully. "You're getting there—but more like this." She shows him.

He tries to hold the pencil, but it disappears in his hand as if it never existed. Papá hardly notices that it's gone until he opens his palm and sees that it's not there! Then his face hardens as Carmen picks up the pencil and puts it in his hand again.

"Look, see," she says. "If you get a grip on it—"

Suddenly his face turns that painful red. His naked, public embarrassment makes me sad.

He cries out, "*Déjeme*. Leave me alone!" Chairs scrape as all turn to look at him.

"*Compañero*—just try . . ." Carmen tries to press his hand around the pencil when all at once he throws the pencil against the wall and his notebook flies onto the floor.

"*¿Qué pasa?*" says Carmen, alarmed.

"I am not a baby that must be taught how to hold something. I am a grown man who farms to grow food for his family. My hands are for work—not for holding pencils."

"*Compañero,*" says Carmen, "you can do it. Just hold on to it."

"You have no idea about anything!" The red of his face pulsates like embers. "No. This is a waste of time!" he says, storming out.

There's silence.

"Perhaps this is enough for tonight," says Carmen when the quiet is too much to bear.

Everyone leaves. This night, the house does not seem large enough for all of us. Carmen sits out of the way until my father marches back inside and signals my mother and they go to bed. Then Carmen tiptoes in, hangs her hammock, and slips into it. Finally when the house is asleep, I take the lantern and go into the outhouse. There, I hold the light up to the newspapers on the walls. I find the *a*'s and the *e*'s and the *i*'s that Carmen was talking about. I make all their sounds until the kerosene burns away and the lantern goes out. Then I have to find my way back to the house in the dark. But I don't mind, because there is another light in my head that illuminates my way.

Zulema Soto

I stare at my name—Z-u-l-e-m-a S-o-t-o—that Carmen has written out on the board.

"Zuh-le-mah Sss-oh-ttt-oh," I whisper, sounding it out, loving the way it looks.

"The next name I write is very special because it is the name of the man of the house who has graciously allowed us to use it!" My father sits in the back of the room, arms folded, gazing out the door.

"Leave me out of it," he grunts.

"Of course," says Carmen. "But we *should* at least do you the honor of writing it down." Then she writes S-a-n-t-i-a-g-o S-o-t-o on the board, sounding out each letter as she goes along. There is silence in the room when she is done.

"That is my name?" Papá whispers in amazement.

"*Sí,*" she answers. "You are Santiago Soto."

He stares at it but suddenly says, "I do not need to know how to write my name. I like using my thumbprint. It has worked for many years."

Carmen moves on and writes Mamá's name: I-s-a-b-e-l S-o-t-o.

"What about you, *compañera*?" she says, turning to Mamá.

"*¿Qué?*" Mamá is amazed.

"This is your name," says Carmen. "What do you think?"

Papá answers for Mamá. "She prefers signing with an *X*."

Mamá shoots him a look before copying her name in her notebook.

By that time, I have written *Zulema Soto* a hundred times in my notebook.

That night, I find the book of fairy tales Ana from Havana gave me. I look at the picture at the beginning of each story and try to sound out the words.

I can make out *apple, pig, dog,* but am I reading? Am I right? Before I know it, I have gone back and forth, over all the stories, picking out words here and there. I feel that reading is like when Mamá wants to comb the tangles out of my hair. She starts at the top of my head and unravels the big tangles until she gets to the bottom. Then she starts at the top again, combing out the smaller tangles. Then she starts again and takes out the smallest tangles, and on and on and on. The tangles are the words I don't understand, so I just keep going to the beginning of the stories to sound them out, to unravel their mysteries.

I write *my* name, Zulema Soto, on the first page of the book so everyone knows the book is mine.

Love Among the Letters

Nilo, Cecilia, and I have run to the end of the village before the community meeting starts. I find a stick and scratch my name in the dirt—*Zulema Soto.*

"Can I try writing my name?" asks Cecilia.

I hand her the stick. She writes the first three letters of her name, then gets stuck.

What a dummy, I think. "I'll show you," I say, writing the rest of her name.

"Write my name under hers," says Nilo, trying to look uninterested. "Looks good," he says when I am done. Then he draws a heart around his and Cecilia's names and looks at her shyly. Cecilia tries to look uninterested as well, but I can tell they are only interested in each other.

"Let's go," I say to remind them that I am there.

"Yes, I'll get us some candy," says Nilo.

We walk back and they lag behind. I'm thinking I don't care about their stupid love affair and speed on ahead when all at once I am forced to stop—because at a certain point, the air begins to shimmer with fear. Suddenly, I feel danger, sucking me toward the store.

I walk faster and faster, then fall into a full-out run!

"What?"

"Huh?"

"Wait!"

Nilo and Cecilia call out—but quickly follow.

I burst in on everyone in the store. They are sharply turning to one another with stricken looks on their faces, hissing questions with no answers.

"Murdered?"

"Killed."

"A *brigadista* has been killed?"

"How can that be?"

"Who would do such a thing?"

"Why?"

"Where?"

"When?"

I look for Carmen and Carlos. They are trying to calm people down. I am relieved they are okay.

"Near the Palmarito Coffee farm," says *el compañero* Linares.

"These are isolated incidents," says Carlos, patting the air calm with his hands. "It happened on the other side of the mountain range very far away. Stay calm."

"An isolated case. That doesn't mean we should stop our classes," says Carmen quickly. And just as quickly our parents call out to us.

"Zulema!" cries Mamá.

"Nilo!" cries out my uncle.

"Cecilia!" cries out Chismosa.

We obey, running into their arms. Once we are accounted for, they continue to talk about the counterrevolutionaries who might have done this terrible thing. I peek at Carmen, who does not look afraid. They all talk and mutter, leaving their worries and concerns in the air until it is time to leave.

Before we ride off with our parents, I find a way to run back to the end of town where Cecilia and Nilo and I had scratched our names into the ground.

I erase our names with my foot in case there are any counter-revolutionaries watching.

Parents

Days later, I feed the chickens, even as I look over my shoulder for danger. Suddenly I hear a car. Do insurgents come in cars? Carmen and Mamá, who are hanging laundry, hear it too. We all three stand on our toes to see. A man and a woman drive up to our house in a yellow car!

Carmen looks over her shoulder and gasps, "Mami? Papi?" She runs over to them. "What are you doing here?"

Mamá and I let our heels settle on the ground again. It's Carmen's parents!

"The question is, What are *you* doing here?" the man answers sternly.

Carmen's mother hugs her, then slides her hands down her daughter's arms. Suddenly she shrieks, turning her daughter's hands over and over in her own. "Look at your hands!" she says. "As rough and red as any common worker's!"

Carmen hides her hands behind her back.

"Never mind about that! What are *you* doing here?" Carmen asks again.

Her father steps forward, hugging her. "We've come to bring you home!" he says sternly. "We heard about some violence against *brigadistas*! This is getting dangerous. Enough of this nonsense! Get your things."

Carmen pulls back. "No, I'm not going home. I am not quitting. We must keep going here. It is important I stay," insists Carmen.

"But why? Who cares if these people learn to read?" says her mother. "You never do what I say!"

Carmen turns to us, red coming through her tan face, coloring her cheeks. "*These people* are my students. This is Zulema and *la compañera* Isabel Soto."

Mamá and I awkwardly walk over to them, smiling. Mamá offers them *café*, which they refuse. My mother then pulls me into the house, but we spy on them from the door.

"She should go home with her parents," whispers my mother. "She should do what they say! They love her. They miss her. Just like I would miss you if you ever went away."

"Where would I go if I ever went away, Mamá?" I ask.

We stare at each other blankly. That question hangs in the air. It has never come up. And if it did, neither one of us would have had an answer.

Carmen and her parents talk some more. Finally her mother and father slump in their yellow car, giving up and driving away. Carmen comes back to the house distracted and suddenly exhausted.

"All right now—where were we?" she says crossly, her brow stormy.

"Chickens and clothes," I say.

"Huh?" says Carmen.

"I was feeding the chickens, and you were hanging the clothes," I say.

Carmen takes a minute. With one rough hand, she wipes her brow free of distraction and confusion and says, "Wait a minute! Let's look at that book Ana gave you!"

I am thrilled and run to get it. We sit on the porch and quickly open it. "Repeat after me: '*Once upon a time . . .*'" says Carmen.

Those little words throw me back to Havana two years ago, and that girl I met named Ana who gave me this book.

In a way, Ana started this whole thing.

River Washing

The water is wonderful today. It's not heavy and monotonous, turning my muscles into ropes, but soft enough to soothe feet and wash clothes—Carmen and I are at this task and have just spread the clothes out on bushes to dry when I begin to take my clothes off.

"What are you doing?" Carmen says, shocked.

"I always take a swim after washing clothes," I say, getting down to my underwear.

She stops, then suddenly says, "If you can do it, I can too!" And takes off her own clothes. Then without another word she steps into the water.

"Careful, Carmen, don't . . . !"

"Whoa!"

Too late! Carmen falls in a deep part of the river. She comes sputtering up! "*¿Qué pasó?*"

"The bottom of the river is uneven," I say. "Be careful."

Suddenly she starts to cry.

"What's the matter?" I ask.

"Nothing. I am just tired and my legs hurt and my arms hurt and . . . all of this is really something," says Carmen, her eyes wide.

"What is?" I say, confused.

"Everything. Washing clothes on rocks like we did, hanging them on branches, going into the river without bathing suits . . . being in pain."

"Come," I say, helping her find her footing and her way to my favorite big rock in the middle of the stream. We hop onto it.

"You are so strong," she remarks, pulling herself up on my arm. "But I guess carrying water every day gave you muscles." She thinks. "Now, I mostly have pain in my arms. But at least the pain tells me where my muscles are," she adds quietly. "I am stronger than my parents think I am. I am not just a little *princesa presumida*, a conceited princess to be stuck in a house all day." Then she stops. "Actually, I didn't know if I was strong at all, until I first saw the signs that said, *Young men and women! Join the army of young literacy workers! The home of a family of peasants who cannot either read or write is waiting for you now! Don't let them down!*

"These signs were all over—that's when I knew just what to do!"

The sun is going down. Shadows cross us. In that coolness I feel free to ask, "How come people don't want me to learn to read?"

"What?"

"The counterrevolutionaries who killed that *brigadista* for teaching? How come they don't want me to learn how to read?"

Carmen sucks in her breath. "Oh, no! It doesn't really have anything to do with *you* learning to read!"

"What, then?"

"Counterrevolutionaries are just against *anything* Fidel Castro thinks of . . ."

"Oh . . ."

"Sometimes I think if Fidel Castro said the sky was blue, some counterrevolutionary would say it wasn't!"

"Oh . . ."

"That's just how it is when people disagree with their emotions instead of their minds."

"Oh . . ."

"And you know, there are always two sides to every story . . ."

"Like water?" I say.

"Water?"

"Yes, sometimes water can be heavy and hateful when I carry it—or wonderful and lovely like it is today!"

Carmen stares at me, then laughs. "I think you are a poet and didn't even know it!"

We gather the clothes and head back.

Counterrevolutionaries

The rain is all things today as I listen to it and practice my letters. Some rain is loud on the tin shed covering the pigs. Some of it is like soft footsteps on the roof. Some is like a waterfall between rocks. The sounds outside blend with those inside, the scratching of pencils, the reciting of letters, the little giggles between Nilo and Cecilia. The patter outside even complements the coughs, the rustling of pages turning, the rough noises of frustration, even the dozing and snoring— it's all the musical tones of writing and reading words.

But our perfect world is interrupted when all at once we hear a galloping horse! After a quick look to each other, Carmen and I creep toward the door to see Carlos jump off his horse and come toward us—the whites of his eyes bulging in the foggy darkness. He pushes us back into the room.

"Stay inside!" he commands.

"*¿Qué pasó?*" asks everybody, his rude and violent entrance shocking everyone.

"Counterrevolutionaries are all over these hills," he says, panting. "They have destroyed some of our camps."

"Destroyed?" says Papá.

"Yes!"

"But who are they?" asks Mamá.

"Who knows? Fanatics," says Carlos.

Papá jumps into action. Maybe his big hands cannot hold a pencil, but they can hold a machete well enough! "Quick! Blow out the lanterns!" he whispers.

Mamá and I blow out all the lanterns.

"But why? Now we can't see!" says Carmen.

"Yes, that is the idea," says Papá, exasperated. "Now the bandits cannot see us either. We don't want them attracted by the light. Everyone, quiet down and stay here. Carlos, you, my brother Zenón, and I will patrol the area."

"I will go too!" says Nilo.

They run out, get on their horses, and ride away.

As the hours pass, the rain lessens, but still drones, wearing some of us down into troubled dozing.

"What do you think is going on?" asks Cecilia nervously.

"It's all right," I say, not knowing if things are all right or not.

"Do you think Nilo will be all right? Nothing can happen to him, right?" she says, big tears glistening in her eyes. I look into them and wonder if it was love that turned her eyes from lizard-like into nice circles of worry. When she reaches for my hand, I surprise myself by letting her take it.

The world is really crazy when Cecilia and I are holding hands!

Safe

We are all in a funny spot between being asleep and awake when daylight comes like a milky-white blanket. Mamá stokes the fire in the *fogón* and brews some coffee. She peeks out the window as we hear horses approaching. "Hand me that frying pan," she whispers.

The men pick up chairs to use as weapons. I grab my broom. Cecilia starts to whimper. "Is it the counterrevolutionaries?" she asks.

"Here, take this," I say, handing her my broom. "If anybody comes in, hit them over the head." I grab another of Mamá's pans and look out the window. "Get back," Mamá says to me, holding her frying pan up above her head.

But I stay to see.

"Whoa," they call out. It is my father, Tío Zenón, Carlos, and Nilo. We deflate with relief. My mother, Tía Lita, and I rush out to meet them.

"We patrolled everywhere. All we saw was the remains of a camp. The counterrevolutionaries left garbage and some empty cans of beans. I think the rain drove them away from this area—the cowards." They come inside where Papá slumps into a chair, exhausted. "Go home, everybody—I think you can all go home now."

"Wait—there is something you should know," says Carlos.

We all turn our heads toward him dumbly.

"Diego and Eladia have changed sides. They have become counterrevolutionaries."

Papa gasps. The room plummets into silence. I look around like an idiot, realizing that Diego and Eladia are not with us. I think of their children. Papa sinks his face into his hands.

Everyone leaves, sleepwalking into the day, melting into the fog, dragging their benches and chairs behind them.

Papá is disgusted and angry. "I knew it, I knew this learning to read and write was dangerous. I never cared about this Revolution. What is wrong with Cubans? Fighting for freedoms and then fighting with one another? I am sick of it."

Carmen is quiet but then defends herself. "I wanted to help the Revolution. I came here to teach, even though my father and mother didn't want me to."

"Nobody asked us *guajiros* what we wanted," says Papá.

"We have broken a lot of old traditions—" Carmen counters.

Papá cuts her off. "There is nothing wrong with traditions."

The rain has finally stopped altogether. The clouds break open, and we feel the warmth of the sun. The room is as quiet as the rain was loud.

"I must go to the fields," says Papá. "The counterrevolutionaries might have done some damage there. I don't know."

Mamá starts to speak. "But—"

"I can rest later," he says sharply. "Stay close to the house today," he commands my mother and me. "You as well, Carmen."

He drinks his coffee. I pour him a jar of water from the clay jug. Water is all I have to give him.

Emergency

There is an emergency community meeting at the general store. "Who is responsible for what happened?" demands my father.

"I don't know," says *el compañero* Linares. "I had not heard of any counterrevolutionaries coming into this area. Everyone here is in accordance with the Revolution."

"Not the people who trampled some of my fields. Who will pay for that? The Revolution?" says Papá.

El compañero Linares looks around nervously. "We will find out. I promise. When you finish your lessons and write to Fidel—"

My father explodes! "There will be no more lessons. It is dangerous! There were bandits out to get us for being in this Campaña Nacional de Alfabetización en Cuba. Are you all not afraid?" There might be counterrevolutionaries among us right now, like Diego and Eladia. This is crazy.

"Perhaps when we write our letters to Fidel, we can complain as *el compañero* Linares suggests," says Chismosa.

"Letters to Fidel! Letters to Fidel! You think writing a letter to Fidel will help?" My father is like the pops of pine sap that escape from burning wood. I want to both run to and away from him.

"Did you not notice what went on here recently?" Papá goes

on. "Counterrevolutionaries were in this mountainside! Look—I don't like these *brigadistas*, but they are innocent young people— and they should not be put in danger because of Fidel!"

"But we don't care about being put in danger," says Carmen. "I mean, of course, we don't want to be put in danger, but we have a job to finish. I have a job to finish."

My father cannot believe his ears. "I want to forget about reading and writing. I want to go back to using my thumbprint."

"But we cannot stop!" says Carmen. "Fidel promised one hundred percent literacy in Cuba in one year!"

"Please, young lady. I am out of this *locura*. Do not tell me what to do. Come back to the house and take down your hammock. I am sorry, but there will be no more reading classes held in my house. Have lessons in someone else's house," he says, throwing his hands up in the air. "I am done with reading and writing. I have to protect my family."

I wish I could fly away from this stupid place.

Retreat

Carmen quietly gathers her things as Carlos waits for her outside.

"I'm sorry," she whispers to me. She looks around, satisfied that she has everything. "I guess that's it."

"What will you do now?" asks Mamá as Papá scowls in a corner.

"Finish the lessons in somebody else's house. Probably Cecilia's house."

"That house is only one room," I say.

Carmen forces a smile. "Yes, it will be cramped and we might be forced to only teach outside, but we will do the best we can until we get the job done."

"The yuca has to be harvested soon," says Mamá.

"We will work around that," she says.

"And then the *plátanos* . . ."

"We'll work around that too," says Carmen, slinging on her backpack. After a final look around the room, she heads for the door.

"Wait, I will get my notebook and go with you," I say.

And Papá, who has not said a word, suddenly says loudly, "Where do you think you are going, Zulema?"

"With Carmen for today's lesson?" I say, confused.

"You cannot go with Carmen to Cecilia's!" he thunders.

"What? Why not?" I say, looking around frantically. I turn to my mother, who looks away.

"Those counterrevolutionaries could be anywhere! They could suddenly show up at Cecilia's house just as easily as they showed up here."

"But—" My face gets hot.

"But nothing! What kind of father would I be if I let you be in danger?"

"But, *compañero*—" says Carmen.

"I am the man of the house! I have to do what is best for my family! Why doesn't anybody understand that?"

"*Pero*, Santiago . . ." says Mamá.

"Good luck, Carmen," says Papá, putting his big, puffy, hateful hand on my shoulder. I collapse, getting out from under it. "Thank you, but we want to go back to normal," he adds.

My mind explodes. Normal what? Normal sweeping the floor, getting water, feeding the chickens, chasing the chickens off the kitchen table, washing clothes normal? I moan as tears rush up. But I shut my face down, stopping them just in time.

"Time to get back to the way things were," says Papá grumpily, going on the porch and lighting his cigar.

Carmen puts her backpack on and joins Carlos outside. They get on their horses. I hold my breath as I watch my last chance vanish around a turn. Mamá goes into the kitchen and begins cutting up the yuca for dinner, as if nothing is different.

"Zulema, can you bring me some water?" calls Papá from the porch.

My tears win my inside battle and burst through—spilling, burning down my face.

Mamá continues chopping.

I rush past Papá's shocked eyes and into the outhouse, where I beat the walls with my fists.

Cheated

From then on, I go into the outhouse even when I don't have to do my business and look at the newspaper on the walls. I find words that are easy to make out.

I read, *Today in Havana*... but then the paper is ripped or pasted over with another paper that says, *In the USA*... but then I can't finish reading that because the rest of those words are pasted over with half of a cartoon that says, *The United Nations*...

I want to know more. I want to know what the rest of everything says. I want to know what the papers say underneath other papers. I want to know things that are beyond my reach.

I have been cheated—betrayed so I could continue to fetch water and feed the chickens and pigs and sweep the dirt floor. My possibilities stolen so people could fight with Fidel about things I didn't even care about.

I just wanted to read! Read and see what was next and under the papers.

"Zulema, where is your mind at?" asks Mamá fearfully.

I don't answer because my mind is everywhere. I sweep the floor and the marks my broom leaves behind make me think of letters. I purposely ignore the poop the chicken leaves on the kitchen table. I don't answer my mother when she calls, because

I have better things to do with my mind until she finally knows to leave me alone.

When I take water to Papá in the field, we avoid each other's eyes and hardly speak. He is not the only one to be grumpy. When he comes back at the end of the day, I don't bring him water like I used to.

One day, he demands a cool drink from me. I bring it as slowly as I can. "Child, why are you being so disrespectful?" he asks, raising his hand as if to give me a knock on the head with his knuckle. I don't even try to get away.

"Santiago!" exclaims my mother, shocked he would even think about giving me a knock on the head.

"Answer me," he insists. He lowers his arm slowly and sits down, looking around like he's lost something. "Why are you being so disrespectful?"

I say nothing.

I don't tell him I feel cheated.

I don't let him know he is a coward.

I swallow it all, like a bitter lime whose juice has stung my tongue.

Showdown

Weeks have passed, but I still wear my anger like a hood. We go to the store. There is an excitement in the air I cannot ignore.

"What's going on, Nilo?" I ask.

"We finished!" he says. "We have passed the reading tests and written our letters to Fidel."

But the most excited is Carmen. "Zulema," she says, finding me through the crowd.

But she is stopped by *el compañero* Linares when he calls out, "Order! Order!" Carmen winks at me and looks toward *el compañero* Linares. "This is a special day. This community has done its part for the Revolution. *Brigadista* Carmen will address you."

My father groans. "What kind of *basura* nonsense do we have to listen to now?"

"Shhh . . ." says Mamá.

My anger at my father thickens.

Carmen, her face pink with happiness, announces, "This is a great day. We have succeeded in—"

"Well, this has nothing to do with me and my family," says Papá like a stupid person, like an ox would say if oxen could talk!

Carmen ignores his interruption. "We have succeeded in teaching everyone." Then she looks at me and my family and adjusts. "Teaching *mostly* everyone in this community to read and write. For all who passed the tests, here are red flags to put on your doors. They will identify your households as being literate!"

"Still telling people what to do, huh?" says Papá nastily.

If Papá says one more thing, I think I will explode!

This time Carmen answers him. "No, not telling you what to do. The red flags will let everyone know of your accomplishment of becoming literate!"

"Everyone take a bow," says Carlos. "And applaud yourselves while you are at it!"

They all applaud and pat one another on the back.

"*¡Bien!*"

"*¡Felicidades!*"

"This is ridiculous," says my father. "Grown people applauding one another."

Oh, why does he have to talk?! Why can't he just shut up!

"I have important things to do!" says Papá. "Like work!"

Yes, like work like an animal! *Doing things oxen can do better,* I think to myself.

"Is anybody here interested in talking about the crops?" my father asks.

Oh, why can't he just stop?! I think loudly in my head.

"Zulema!" says Papá, loud enough so everyone looks at him sternly.

Oh, why can't he just shut up?!

"Let's go!"

All at once, and from a place I didn't know I had, way down

deep inside, I explode. "What? What do you want!" I screech. "Why do you have to stop everything that's good? Why does everything have to be your way? Why can't I read? What are you afraid of?!"

My father is stunned. He sucks in his breath in anger. Everyone is looking at me. At him. My father raises his hand to slap me. Panicking, I grab a comic book off the rack and hold it above my head. He knocks it out of my hand, but I pick it up—and turn to the first page.

Read

I read the title. *"Adventures of R-Real L-Life."*

My heart is beating so loudly in my ears I can hardly hear myself, but I go on making sounds of the letters I see.

"Our hero F-Fernando is in the wilds of Africa l-looking for lost gold."

I am amazed I know those words! I continue, *"Suddenly, from out of nowhere, Fernando hears a growl."* How can I know those words? How come the letters and sounds are falling into place? I look to my father's brokenhearted face and speak to him directly. "See. I read, and nothing happened. Nobody died. No counterrevolutionaries showed up!"

"Zulema, let's go home," he says weakly.

"No," I say, and bury my head in the comic to read further. *"His heart starts to beat."*

The hot tears that come to my eyes blur the words on the page, so I wipe them away. I must keep reading because now I know the truth. I hate my father's old-fashioned ways. And I will show him how much I hate his ways by spitting the words I read right at him.

"Sweat b-breaks out on his forehead." I feel sweat breaking out on my forehead too!

"The hairs on the back of his head stand up!" I will stand up

for myself, just like this stupid Fernando guy I'm reading about does!

"*S-suddenly the tiger pounces. His claws dig into Fernando's chest and begin to rip.*"

I stop to catch my breath.

"Wow!" says Nilo. "You read better than me!"

"Me too," says Cecilia.

My father looks lost. My mother goes near him but sends her strength to me, like she is a bridge between us.

"Read more!" says Carmen.

"*The tiger growls. Fernando can feel its hot breath smelling of damp earth. Fernando reaches for his knife strapped to his loincloth. He drives his knife into the tiger's eye! Blood spurts all over.*"

"Eww," exclaims everybody at once.

"*Fernando continues to stab the beast until it's dead.*"

All I have to do now is finish. "*So Fernando, our hero, contin-contin-ues continues his thirst for gold, making it possible for him to kill whatever stands in his way.*"

Everybody applauds.

Carmen turns to my father. "*Compañero* Soto, this is wonderful! This is proof of how our reading initiative has succeeded. Your daughter has learned to read even though she didn't have as much practice as everyone else."

Then she says, slowly and calmly and seriously, "Your daughter is a fine example of the Revolution."

"It is a miracle," says el *compañero* Linares.

"Not a miracle," says Carlos. "It is the Revolution!"

More clapping.

"Red flags for everyone, including you, Zulema!" Carmen and Carlos give out red flags as everyone talks about reading and writing. Their voices rise and fall around me. My mother looks at me proudly. I finally have the nerve to look at my father, who turns away.

All the way home we are quiet.

The sound of the *carreta*'s wheels turning is all we hear.

I try to hide my flag underneath my dress. It seems to burn against my thigh the way the magazine Nilo stole for me did.

Papá's Problem

It feels as if my house is on an edge, trying to balance and not snap, but we all snap anyway. Mamá snaps at Papá, Papá snaps at Mamá. The pigs snap at the chickens, the chickens snap at the pigs. I snap at the chicken on the table.

One night I return from rereading the half sentences of old news on the outhouse walls to read my book of fairy tales. It's a little harder to read than the outhouse walls, so I like it better. I know all the words in the magazine Nilo stole for me by heart.

I see Papá's shape as he sits on the porch, chewing on his evening cigar, slumped, as if his legs were broken. The curve in his back softens my anger.

He says, *"Agua."* But it sounds like a request and not a command. I get him a jar of water, which he clutches in his big paw hands. I wonder how painful it is for him to hold a jar.

Finished, he hands me the jar and I see thick dirt under his nails, and I am reminded that his hands hold a plow so we can eat and a machete so he can protect us. I turn to go, but instead stop and ask, "What's the matter, Papá?"

He makes believe he doesn't hear me, so I ask him again. He takes a breath and answers, "I don't know."

Mamá comes to the door.

"Are you angry because I can read?" I ask.

Mamá tiptoes away.

He stands up, shocked. "No! How can you say such a thing?"

"The way you were at the store weeks ago. I just thought . . ."

"No . . ." He sits back down and slumps, before he asks, "How old are you?"

"Almost twelve."

He sighs. Then looking all confused he says, "All these changes."

"I can't help growing . . ." I say.

"No, no, not you. I know you must grow. I mean all the changes in Cuba. All the changes around me." He goes on, trying to explain. "I like farming because it's the same thing every year. But the Revolution has changed everything."

"Don't you like it?"

"What?"

"That the Revolution has changed everything?"

My father thinks. Then he says, "No. I don't like it." His own answer surprises him. Then he thinks some more. "Because I can't change."

I let his words settle into me like rain in sand.

Then he asks, "Where is your red flag?"

"Under my bed," I answer.

"Why don't you hang it?"

"Because the whole family has to know how to read and write in order for me to hang it. Not just me."

He says nothing. But I see an idea in the distance that keeps coming at me as the night wears on.

My Plan

The next day, when Papá goes outside to smoke, I tell Mamá what I'm thinking. She listens, then suddenly agrees. Now all I have to do is share my idea with him. Mamá and I join him on the porch. Papá is surprised to see her there.

"What are you doing out here, woman?" he asks Mamá.

"Aren't you afraid of the *sereno* air?" he teases.

"I guess not," she says. "It's an old-fashioned idea. I've changed my mind about it," she adds gently.

"What's going on with you two?" Papá asks suspiciously.

"Your daughter has something to say," Mamá says.

Papá takes a puff on his cigar.

"I want to be a teacher," I say.

"What?" he says, taking a bigger puff.

"I want to be a teacher."

"Like a *brigadista*?"

"No, like a *real* teacher who teaches in a school."

"What school?"

"Carmen said—"

"Bah," he says.

I go on before he can say anything more. "Carmen said schools will be built in the countryside soon. I will be ready to teach in them, in a few years when they *are* here. But I need your help." I look to Mamá. "Both of you."

"I need your help practicing teaching. I need to practice on you two."

Papá lets it sink in and then laughs. "You'll have more luck if you practice on one of the pigs."

"That's not funny, Papá," I say.

"Look," he answers. "I would help if these hands could hold a pencil," he sighs. "Practice on someone else."

I feel hurt for him, so I cover it up by saying, "No—I think I should practice on you two."

He turns his whole body to me.

"Zulema, I am too old to learn to read and write. My fingers are too thick with work to hold a pencil, my mind too cloudy with old ideas to learn anything new. Practice on your mother. I give my permission."

"No," says Mamá. "You are the man of the house. If she can't practice on you, she cannot practice."

We leave it there.

Working on Papá

It takes me weeks to convince him.

"All right! All right," he finally says, trying to hide a grin. "My goodness, you are like the flies that torment the oxen. Worse!"

Mamá goes first. The best time to share what I know with Mamá is when we are hanging clothes or preparing dinner. It seems to be working.

I try to talk to Papá about sounds and letters when I take water to him, but that's not a good idea at all. A good time for him is after dinner.

"Again?" he says, sitting down, making believe he is shocked. "We did this last night!"

"Yes," I say. "We have to go over the letter sounds again."

But the best time for us is when we practice writing. Because it is still hard for him to hold a pencil, we take long breaks, and in those long breaks, we talk.

He says, "You know, my mother had big hands like me, but still, she was able to crochet."

"Crochet?

"*Sí*, so silly to have a doily in a room with a dirt floor, but there it was, a lovely *tapete* as pretty as any spider's web. She died when I was a boy, but I remember the way her hands felt."

"Did they feel like big, fat, rough pillows?" I ask.

His eyes get wide. "What . . . ? Huh? How did you know?"

I hold his hands. "Because that's how your hands feel to me."

"Yes, they were rough and calloused on the outside, but somehow soft inside." He turns away, his eyes glistening. "Let's get back to work," he whispers.

On another day, I ask him about his father.

"Oh . . . he loved your mother almost more than he loved me," he says jokingly. "He was very happy when I asked your mother to marry me. He didn't want me to be alone."

Over the days and weeks, he practices and tells me little things. "My father was very gruff, but he always left a little extra yuca on his plate for me so I would know how much he loved me. And when we roasted a pig every Christmas, he always gave me the crispiest crackling." And, "You'd think I was the last child on earth during hurricane season when he made me stay in the *varentierra* safe house until he was sure the storm was over."

And in this mixture of storytelling and letters and writing, it takes Papá a month and a half to learn well enough to read a little and be able to write his name and some words.

Mamá only took one month to learn. "Don't tell your father," she had whispered to me on the day it was clear she knew enough to pass the test.

"But why?" I had asked, confused.

"I just . . . I can't say, but I don't want your father to feel bad."

"Why should he feel bad?"

"I don't want him to think I am smarter than he is," she had added, smiling.

When my father is ready, I get word to Carmen through *el compañero* Linares at a community meeting.

Test

Of course, we all pass the test.

"Zulema," says Carmen. "You did something I could not do! Teach your parents! You are a good teacher."

I turn away, a little embarrassed, especially when this is how Papá writes his letter to Fidel Castro:

Dear compañero:
I used to be illiterate. I am writing you so you can see that I know how to read and write. But it was my daughter who really taught me. You, my so-called compañero, are a crap eater.
Santiago Soto

We decide to take the "my so-called *compañero*" and "crap eater" part out before we send it to Fidel. I think Papa knew we would. Carmen gathers my mother's letter and my own when she stops and looks at me seriously. "Thank you."

"For what?"

"For helping me get through it all and not fall apart."

I laugh.

She turns to go—stops—then turns back. "Do you remember Ana?"

"Ana from Havana? Of course, from the Havana rally," I say.

"She gave me my first book!"

"Remember I told you she sent me a letter?"

I nod.

"I never read it to you." Carmen pulls out the letter. "But I'll read it now." She reads:

"Dear Carmen,

By the time you read this, I will be gone. You must understand, with Papi dead we cannot be in Cuba. We cannot be in a place that loves Fidel Castro. I don't know how we could have let a stupid politician's ideas come between us, but we have."

Carmen looks at me for a moment before going on.

"I hope you find something good in this country. For now, I do not. Your ex-friend, Ana."

She folds the letter carefully and puts it away. "I never wrote back to her because she made me mad. But also because I didn't have a good answer about what was good in this new Cuba. But now I know one thing that's good."

"What?" I ask.

"You," she answers. "You are a good thing to be found in this country." With that, she gives me a hug and goes away.

I never see Carmen again, but I think of her whenever I see Mamá and Papá reading a newspaper before using it as wallpaper in the outhouse. Or Mamá reading *Bohemia* magazine every now and then too. She moves her lips as she reads—but she is reading!

Papá won't read propaganda, but I know he is happy he can write because he stands up a little taller when he signs his name on some kind of business at the store, instead of pressing his finger on a pad. Sometimes I can hear my parents sounding out words in the outhouse.

Of course, I think of Carmen every time I look at the little red flag she gave us to put up on our house to announce we are literate. I step back to see how the flag waves gaily in the breeze and make a mental note that flags move while staying in one place.

Final Moment

Nilo rolls up his pants and I hold up my dress as we wade out to my favorite rock in the river. I tell him all the things Carmen told me about trying new things in life. He listens and nods all the way out to the rock. I wait until he is settled to tell him my life plan of becoming a teacher.

"A teacher?" he says. "Good for you! You always were a smart aleck, telling people what to do. Now you can boss little kids around!"

"What will *you* do?" I ask, guessing he'll say a teacher like me, or a representative for the government or something.

"Me? What do you mean? I'm going to be a farmer, like my father."

I am surprised at his answer. "Why?"

"Why? Because I like farming! I have always liked farming!"

"But it's the same thing all the time, every day!" I say.

"That's why I like it," he answers.

"But . . ."

"But nothing." He smiles.

"But I'm going to be a teacher," I repeat weakly.

"So be a teacher . . ." he answers, chewing on a piece of grass he had picked up along the way.

"I can't believe you are not going to do anything else!" I say.

"But I am going to do something else—I am going to marry Cecilia."

"What?!" I almost fall off and plop in the water like Carmen did.

"I mean, when we both grow up, of course," he adds.

"But . . . why?" I sputter.

"There's something about the way she eats candy. I can watch her eat candy all day," he says.

The *brigadistas* are long gone. Our red flag announcing that we are literate has faded in the beautiful sun that comes and goes.

Sometimes, when I go to wash clothes, I look at the river flowing away and suddenly I feel sad. I know I will leave this place to be a teacher somewhere, someday, I just know it. But it makes me so sad to think about maybe leaving Papá and Mamá behind, and a tear falls down my face and joins the water.

But then I look at the river that moves all the time while staying in the same place, like the flag that waves in the wind but stays in the same place. I think that I am not really going away—I am just moving like that river. But like the river, in my heart, I will also always stay here, in my beloved Cuba.

To change masters is not to be free.

—JOSÉ MARTÍ

Juan

HAVANA, CUBA • 1961

I stick a pin in my finger.

"Does it hurt, Juan?" Paco asks me.

"No," I say, sticking it in a little farther.

"Ewww," says Paco.

I dig the pin in until blood pops, and then I squeeze out a perfect little red bubble. After wiping the pin on my pants, I hand it to Paco. He looks at the pin. I look at the ball of blood on the tip of my finger.

"Come on, before the blood gets hard," I say as gently as I can.

Paco looks at it, then says, "I can't do it, Juan."

Quickly, I suck out the blood, which tastes like metal. "Then let's not do it," I say. It's no good if you have to force someone to be your blood brother. They have to *want* to. "Don't worry, Paco, this isn't the right time. When the right time comes, we'll do it."

The sun just going down over Havana Harbor makes pink and yellow light slip through the clouds. The spilling light turns everything rosy-gold: our mangy brown neighborhood, the trash piled up in the base of the palm trees, the tips of the palm leaves in the trees, our dark skin.

Paco suddenly turns to me. "Okay, wait—I'll do it!"

"Are you sure?" I ask. "I don't want to force—."

"*Sí,*" he answers. "I'm sure."

"Doubly sure?"

"Yes!" he says.

"Triple sure?" I press.

"*Sí,*" he answers.

I try to give him the pin.

"*You* stick me," he says.

"No. You have to stick yourself," I say.

He pauses.

"Now, if you are not ready . . ." I add.

"I'm ready, I'm ready," he says quickly. He closes his eyes and starts to jab at his finger.

"It's better if you do it with your eyes open," I suggest, teasing him just a very little bit.

Paco presses his lips together into a half smile. And finally, after a few tries, he pokes his finger deep enough so a tiny bit of blood escapes. By this time my blood has quit coming so I stick my finger again, for a fresh red bubble. We take a deep breath . . . then press our bloody fingers together.

"Now we are blood brothers, always united, even though we have different mothers and fathers," I say.

Paco looks at me seriously.

"From this day on, we will always look out for each other, no matter what," I add.

But it feels as if I should say something else. "In the name of the Father and the Son and the Holy Ghost," I offer. "Now you say something."

"What?" says Paco.

"Something serious," I say.

He says, "In the name of the Father and the Son and the Holy Ghost" too.

I think for a minute and then add, "And in the name of Africa and all the orisha saints that protect us."

"Anybody else?" asks Paco.

"No, I think it's enough," I say.

Suddenly Paco grins. "Cool, man!"

Then, as if one of the higher powers we swore on heard us, a breeze blows away all the clouds. We are in the few seconds before darkness when the stars wink their way hello.

¡Frutas, naranjas dulces!

It's my *abuelo*'s sweet voice singing about his fruit for sale, and with Paco's arm over my shoulder, we stroll out of the harbor to find him.

Just like brothers who will always look out for each other.

Pioneros

Arriba, abajo
Los yanquis son guanajos
Up, down, Americans are fools

My fake wooden gun jams into my hip, and I am getting pretty sick and tired of marching around the schoolyard saying, "Americans are fools" over and over again when I never even met any Americans. I'm only doing this because of Paco.

"Hey, Juan," Paco calls out, marching next to me. "You are out of step. What kind of rebel soldier are you anyway?" He grins.

"No kind of rebel soldier," I whisper back. Then I stick my tongue out at him. I hate these drills. Since Fidel resisted the Yankees in the Bay of Pigs attack, he wants to make a soldier out of everyone. What am I going to do—beat the American army back with this stick if they return? I feel my mouth, dry as dust—so I give Paco a look that says, *I'm dying of thirst.* Paco gives me a look that says, *Okay, we're almost done.*

Sweating, I pull my *Pionero* neckerchief off so quickly it gets caught on my nose.

This makes Paco laugh. "Ha-ha! That's what you get for being out of step—a neckerchief up your nose!"

"This feels like a noose," I say.

"Aww, come on," chuckles Paco. "It's not that bad. The neckerchiefs are cool and let everybody know we are *pioneros*."

Arriba, abajo

Los yanquis son guanajos

After three more marches around the yard, finally (but not soon enough), the instructor calls out, "That's enough for today! Class dismissed!"

Everyone races to return their fake rifles to the bin.

"Come on," says Paco, pulling on me. "We better hurry up if we're going to get you a sip of water." Dropping our rifles off, we run to the water fountain inside—but the line is already long with kids who are *not pioneros*, who got here before us. After shooting me a quick grin, Paco calls out, "Emergency, emergency! Juan is going to faint if he doesn't get water!" Then he turns to me, whispering, "Look like you are going to faint!"

He's silly, but I go along. The kids laugh and get out of our way. At the fountain, Paco holds the spigot down for me. "Drink fast!" he whispers. "Like you were really dying or they'll know we were faking."

I wipe my mouth. "Paco—they know we're faking. That's why they are laughing at us." But he's already on to the next thing we do.

"On your mark, get set, go!" he screams.

We grab our book bags and run to the plaza. I am always two steps ahead of Paco because my legs are so long, but still— we are in perfect sync, like two birds swooping, then turning on a dime, looking for the ice-cream man. When we see him, we steer our flying feet and come in for a perfect landing. Then we dig into our pockets.

"How much do you have?" I ask Paco.

Paco turns his pockets inside out, then holds out a mixture of Cuban and American money, some lint, and a button. Then I pull out what I've got. We have just enough for two cones.

"I'll have a coconut ice-cream cone," says Paco to the ice-cream man.

"Make mine a pineapple," I add.

We get our cones, and we lick them as we walk around going nowhere. The world is ours to look at. Tiny chunks of pineapple leave a scratchy sweetness on my tongue. I know the strings of coconut feel chewy on Paco's tongue.

Some ice cream drips down Paco's chin, and I know how ice cream looks as it drips down my chin because we are mirror images of each other. We have the same soft, spongy hair and lion-flaring nostrils. When we've eaten half, we switch cones and lick them down until there is nothing left but sticky fingers.

Diving

"Paco, take my rifle," I say one day after the drill. "I want to dive."

"Okay," he says. "I'll meet you at the harbor."

Racing away from school, I practically fly through the streets of my crooked neighborhood. I can almost run with my eyes closed, because I know exactly where the cracks and the holes in the sidewalk are and can skip over the boards that cover the stinking puddles that never dry up.

Finally I get to the pink house with the room I share with my *abuelo*. Opening the gate, I push myself in, peeling off my sticky white shirt and light brown shorts even as I go, pulling at the neckerchief that always takes time as the knot tightens with the sweat I put into it. Looking in the mirror so I can see, watching my fingers loosen the neckerchief, I finally shake it off. Pulling on everyday shorts, I run out to the harbor—free!

The ferry is filling with people. Someone throws a coin in the water. Sending a small hope to the orisha saint of water, *Yemayá*, I jump in! Splash! Like a knife I dive through the rainbow-colored oil floating on top of the water and catch the coin before it flips and turns and tumbles, over and over on itself. I catch the coins other people throw in.

Holding the coins up above my head, I see Paco on the dock. His "thumbs-up" look makes me want to dive harder and deeper. When I come up, I grin, which makes the passengers throw even more coins.

In the yellow part of the water, where the sun still shines through, I see the ferry boat propeller pushing the water—*swoosh-swoosh*—making the boat move. My legs can paddle hard, but not like that. I look at how the propeller works as long as I can, but then the hurt in my lungs that begs for air makes me pop up like a cork!

I use my propeller legs to kick my way back to the dock and my blood brother.

"You were great," says Paco. "You swim so strong! You look like a *tiburón*—a shark."

He gives me a hand, pulling me up out of the water. "Thanks!" I shake off the oil and gasoline that sit right on the top of my hair.

"Whoa, you're getting it all on me!" he laughs, stepping back. "I don't want that oil in my hair. I use *brillantina* on my hair." He laughs again. Then he adds, "How much you got?"

I open my palm. We count. "I might have some left over for ice cream after I show Abuelo," I say.

"Okay," he says. "But I got some money too . . . from my parents. They left me some," he says flatly.

Frutas, naranjas dulces . . .

My *abuelo*'s beautiful voice fills the air.

"Come on," I say.

We run to Abuelo and his fruit cart a little ways away. As I run, I cock my head to one side and feel some warm oily water drip out of my ears.

Abuelo

Abuelo's voice is sweeter than all the fruit he is selling, sweeter than any mango or pineapple or papaya I have ever eaten in my whole life. He stops singing the minute he sees us and smiles.

"*Hola*, Juan, *hola*, Paco."

"Abuelo Segundo, I got a lot of money!" I call out. "Look," I say, showing him. Abuelo squints into my hand. "Can you see?" The thin white skin growing over Abuelo's dark eyes makes them look blue.

"Yes, I can see the coins well enough," he says, pushing them around in my hand with his rough, round fingertip. "But if I can feel the coins with my finger, it's as if I can see them *better*!"

"Do we have enough money for rice and eggs?" I ask.

"Almost," he says, taking off his straw hat and scratching his head. His gray hair looks like little circles of white clouds floating around, just barely hanging on. He coughs, then turns away from us and spits. "We will be all right," he adds. His breathing sounds as if he has a whistle in his chest. "In fact, take some money back for ice cream for you and Paco," he adds, smiling at Paco as he hands me a few coins.

"We'll get ice cream tomorrow," I say. "I have to help Abuelo push the cart home."

"Let's go," says Abuelo. Then he turns to Paco. *"Adiós,* nice to see you, Paco."

But Paco doesn't turn to go home. Instead he helps us cover the cart. When the cart is covered, Abuelo says, *"Hasta mañana,* Paco."

But it's as if Paco has gone deaf because he grabs the handles of the cart, and with head down and shoulders tense with effort, Paco begins to push. Abuelo and I look at each other and shrug. I help Paco. Once we've gone a ways, Abuelo abruptly says, "Let's cross the street here."

Looking up, I see why—Abuelo has spied a Committees for the Defense of the Revolution office. The sign out front has its initials—CDR—and also, a *Viva la Revolución* sign that somebody wrote on a board with a felt-tip pen. The CDR man is sitting outside, smoking a cigarette—watching.

"Don't look at him," says Abuelo. "I hate these neighborhood guys always spying on us," he adds under his breath.

"But that's Nelson, our old garbage collector," says Paco.

Abuelo peers. "Hey, you are right. It *is* him! I didn't recognize him with my frosty eyes."

"Our teacher says the neighbors who have joined the CDRs are the 'eyes and ears' of the Revolution," adds Paco.

"I'll tell you what they are," says Abuelo, looking away. "Nosy neighbors who like to spy on people, that's all! I think I'll call him Nosey Nelson from now on. Blind followers don't deserve real names."

We try to push on, unnoticed. When we get to my pink house, we say good-bye to Paco for a third time.

"See you tomorrow, Paco."

But he starts to pick paint chips off the gate.

"Why don't you come by early tomorrow so we can play ball before school, okay?" I add.

"Sure," he says finally.

Then he looks around, picks up a palm frond, and wanders off—sweeping it along the gates on his way home.

"There goes a lonely boy," says Abuelo, looking after him.

"Why do you say that?"

"He didn't want to go home," says Abuelo, surprised I didn't see that myself. I look down the street but just miss him as he turns the corner.

Housemates

"*¿Café?*" offers Mizcladia the minute we walk into the kitchen we share, pink rollers all over her head. Her daughter, Perfidia, plays on the tile floor with a tiny Matchbox toy car from America. Tightly holding it in her fat little hand, she runs it back and forth on the tile. The noise fills the room.

"*No, gracias,*" says Abuelo. "We'll make our own *café* after dinner."

"You have to let the car go," I tease Perfidia. She is so pretty as she tries to figure me out with her four-year-old eyes. "Look!" I say, kneeling down and showing her. "Like this," and I push the car forward gently, letting it smash into the refrigerator. Perfidia's eyes get wide as a giggle builds inside her. "You try it," I say. She concentrates so hard her eyebrows come together as her two-tone lips push out. Then she propels the car forward again and again, laughing every time it smashes into something. We play for a while until her family leaves the kitchen to Abuelo and me.

Abuelo and I wash up before we cook. "Just simple seasoning, Juan," he says. "Don't insult the fish with too much salt and pepper." He hums as I flavor the fish perfectly.

After dinner, we try to watch television, but give up—Fidel has taken over all the television stations, and all there is to watch is *him* giving speeches. Abuelo's head falls onto his chest, asleep. That's one thing Fidel is good for, I think—putting Abuelo to sleep.

I help get him into bed. Then I light the candles on the altar above our door to the *orisha* saints so the blue-and-green glass in the fan lights reflect a beautiful glow. I make sure the cigar left for the saints is still fresh, and I pray that I will not forget my parents, even though their memory is getting weaker and weaker every year.

"Why do you think Paco is lonely, Abuelo?"

"You would know better than I. You are his best friend," says Abuelo, snorting awake.

"But how can he be lonely? He has me," I say.

"People are lonely for many reasons."

"And we are *more* than friends. We are blood brothers—even though he likes being a *pionero*," I add reluctantly.

"Friends don't have to like the same things," he says, then he begins to cough. While I wait for him to stop, I sneak in a wish to the *Babalú Ayé orisha* that his cough would go away, and then I say, "I still hate being a *pionero*."

"Shhh," says Abuelo quickly, then he lowers his voice as if the walls had ears. "Don't let anyone hear you say that," he warns. "You never know who you're talking to . . ."

"But—"

"No buts. Since the Bay of Pigs mess, Fidel's people are everywhere. Learn to be careful." And with that he turns away—a series of flutter farts signaling uneasy sleep."

Paco

School. I look closely into Paco's eyes for signs of loneliness, but he seems the same as always. Even while handing me a drawing of a rebel soldier shooting a man in the butt who is carrying an American flag. "Here's my impression of the Bay of Pigs," he snickers.

I laugh, whispering, "Very funny, Paco. Now stop before the teacher sees us." But I am glad he is joking around again.

Paco sits back and when I am sure he is not looking at me, I sneak another peek at him. This time he looks miserable. When he sees I've caught him, he grins and throws a piece of wadded paper at my head.

"A gear is just a wheel with teeth," says the teacher.

Paco whispers, "Juan . . . ?"

"What?" I whisper, trying to keep an eye on the teacher.

"Do you want to come over later?"

"*Sí*, why not?" I whisper back.

"Quiet," says the teacher.

"Okay, great . . ." says Paco.

"*Silencio,* you two . . ." says the teacher more urgently. "Now, as I was saying before Paco and Juan interrupted me—a gear is just a wheel with teeth." I sit up in my seat.

Gears killed my parents. I actually think bicycle gears snapped their necks. They were riding a two-person bicycle, going to a place called Coney Island in Brooklyn, in the United States of America, when a truck delivering fish smashed into them. They were found in a mess of mangled gears up around their necks. Since then, I have always wanted to know about gears.

Anyway, I still like fish.

The teacher goes on, "It takes two wheels with teeth that are called cogs to engage for gears to work."

Paco leans over to me. "We can do whatever we want when we get to my house," he whispers. "Play dominos, or dice, or checkers . . ."

"Juan! Paco! Would you two like to continue your conversation outside?" scolds the teacher. "It's almost noon. Maybe the hot sun will make you be quiet!"

"No—I'm sorry, teacher," I say, fake glaring at Paco.

"You two shouldn't sit so close together. For your own good, Paco, come sit by me," the teacher adds.

Paco picks up his book bag and moves to the front of the class as everyone giggles.

I give Paco a look that says, *See what happens when you fool around so much.*

And he gives me a look that says, *What did I do? I can't help it!*

Then I mouth, *You talk as much as a crazy parrot!*

He flaps his arms like wings! "Paco!" yells the teacher. "Outside!" And when he shoots me a grin, I am fooled into thinking he's all right.

Stinky Home

The garbage smell in Paco's apartment is so bad I don't know what to say, so I blurt out, "You almost got me kicked out of class."

"That class is boring," he says.

"You think all classes are boring . . ." I add weakly, trying to figure out where to point my nose to escape the bad smells everywhere.

The three-room apartment Paco lives in with his parents looks like a hurricane hit it. The pillows are half on and off the bed. All the kitchen cabinet doors are open. There are open cans of food on the counters, and the sink is piled high with dirty dishes. I even think I see a green lizard slide over them. Paco avoids my eyes.

"Where are your parents?" I ask.

"Committee meetings," says Paco quickly.

"How long have they been gone?" I ask.

"One week and three days, but they'll be home soon, almost any . . . minute." The words are thick in his throat.

"You're lying," I say quietly.

We lock eyes, and just as suddenly he begins to cry.

"Paco, what's wrong?"

"My parents have been gone two weeks. They keep

saying they're coming back, but they don't. I don't know what to think . . ." His sobs gently rock his body.

"Why didn't you tell me?" I say.

"I didn't want you to think I was a baby."

"What?"

"I said I didn't want you to think I was a baby. What kind of rebel soldier cries for his mami?" Paco goes on, "I don't want to let my parents down."

"But we're blood brothers," I say.

"I know," he sniffles. "But they're my parents," and he begins sobbing again.

"Let's go outside," I say after a while.

We toss a ball back and forth in front of his house until it gets dark.

"Do you really think your parents will come home tonight?" I ask.

"I don't know," he answers miserably.

We play until it's time for me to get home to dinner. "I'm supposed to be home by now," I say.

Paco's face falls. "Can't you stay a little longer?" he almost begs.

"Abuelo is waiting," I say. "I'll see you tomorrow, okay?"

"Okay, I'll pick you up for school," he says quickly.

I nod. "We'll go to the dump soon. Want to?" I add.

"Okay," he says.

My stomach rumbles as I turn away, and I can't help wondering what Paco is going to eat for dinner. I turn back to him. "Hey, you got any food in the house?"

"I think I have an egg," Paco says quietly. "See you tomorrow."

"Okay," I say.

"I'll come by early . . ." he adds, double-checking our plan.

"Extra early," I say. I can feel his eyes on me. When I get to the end of the street and look back, he waves.

I yell, "Come home with me for dinner!"

Paco runs at me like a shot. When we get near my house, Abuelo is looking for me in the darkness. "Juan?"

"Home, Abuelo," I announce. "Paco is going to eat with us!"

"*Bien,*" he says, patting my head before kissing it. We go inside and I show Paco a Slinky, a Hula-Hoop, and some marbles I had found at the dump. "We'll go to the dump soon and find more stuff, okay?"

"Yeah," says Paco happily.

And we have dinner, and after Paco goes home, and as I help Abuelo into bed, I can't help feeling lucky because I have one Abuelo who can't wait to see me, instead of two parents who are always at committee meetings.

Abuelo snores and flutter farts in agreement.

Nosey Nelson

Once I've seen Paco's sadness, he does not try to hide it. I keep him busy at the dump. "Look, Paco," I say, showing him a find: an old juicer. "I think I can fix it."

Paco scratches a mosquito bite.

I see an old mattress. "Hey, Paco, you know how performers jump up and down on trampolines? I bet we can do that too!"

"Huh?"

"Come on, let's try!"

Paco sighs. "I don't know . . ."

"Come on," I say, running to the mattress. "Don't be like that!"

Paco starts to grin just a little.

"I bet I can jump higher than you because of my longer legs!"

That gets Paco going. "Oh, you and your legs!" he adds, teasing and joining me on the mattress.

I go higher. Then he goes higher. Then I go higher. Then Paco goes higher still.

"Wheee!" he finally screams as he jumps way up into the air. But when he lands, his foot goes right through a rotten part of the mattress and through the springs below.

"See what you get," I tease. "I told you I could jump higher than you!" When he doesn't answer, I know he is hurt.

"Let me see," I say.

Paco untangles his leg carefully. His knee had caught on the metal underneath and is now a bloody mess.

"That needs Mercurochrome. Does your mother keep any in the house?" I ask.

I shouldn't have mentioned his mother. Paco's face scrunches small like paper curls up in a fire. He cries openly, but no sound comes out.

A sharp voice cuts through the air. "Hey, you boys—what are you doing over there?" It's Nosey Nelson, the CDR man. Paco and I look down and make believe we don't hear him. "Come on over here!" he demands.

We don't dare not go. I help Paco limp over.

"What happened?" he asks, eyeing Paco's cut knee.

"Nothing," says Paco. "I just cut myself playing."

"You better have your mother put some Mercurochrome on that cut," he says.

That gets him crying all over again. "She's not home," he says. "She's at a committee meeting somewhere. My father too."

Nosey Nelson watches us, then says, "You shouldn't cry about that, little man. Your parents are working for the Revolution. There is no greater cause!"

Suddenly I wish I hadn't gotten up this morning.

Paco gulps mouthfuls of air. "I . . . know . . . but . . ."

"There's a get-together at the youth center—why don't you two come? We can put some Mercurochrome on that cut knee." He turns away, and when we don't follow quick enough, he turns back saying, "Wouldn't you like to come?"

But it doesn't sound like an invitation. It sounds like a command.

"Come on, let's go! We'll fix up your knee . . ."

We don't say anything.

"And you can learn more about the Revolution. You want to do that, don't you?"

What could we do but nod yes.

"You want your parents to be proud of you when they return, don't you?" His hot breath presses against us but he focuses on Paco. "You want to impress them with all the facts you've learned, right?"

I knew that could never happen. Paco never learned a fact in his life. His school grades proved it. All at once, Nelson becomes all syrupy and sweet. "There will be lots of *croquetas* at the center. You can eat as you learn."

"*¿Croquetas . . . ?*" says Paco. It's as if his head cannot understand the Revolution and ham-filled cheese balls exist in the same world.

"Plenty of *croquetas*," adds Nosey, licking his lips. "Come on, I'll give you a piggyback ride," and he wrestles Paco onto his back. "Let's go!" he says. Then he looks at me and says, "You too."

And there is nothing I can do but follow.

Food

The rumba music at the youth center is so loud I cannot think! There are about ten kids our age, some from school and some not, and some older kids, dancing.

"Let's go bandage that knee!" screams Nelson.

Passing a lady carrying a steaming tray of *croquetas*, Paco turns, but Nelson pulls him back. "Don't worry, there's plenty of food. Let's take care of your leg!"

Everyone else grabs at the food until there is nothing left but greasy napkins.

"Don't worry," says the lady, eyeing me. "I'll bring more!"

"Did I miss the food?" says Paco, coming out with a bandaged knee. "Where's the food?" he asks, sniffing the air. And like magic, more food appears. The lady holds the tray right under Paco's nose. His eyes get as round and big as the *croqueta* he grabs. "*Ayyy,*" he sighs, stuffing one in his mouth even as he tries to cool it as it sits on his tongue.

He eats, kids dance and stand around, and then a Fidel speech recording comes on. "Let's go, Paco," I urge.

"No, wait a minute," he answers.

"Come on, you can't possibly eat any more."

"How do you know . . . ?"

The lady comes out with pieces of pineapple on sticks, tempting everyone.

I wait until she turns away before I say, "Come on, Paco. Abuelo has better fruit than this. Let's go."

"But it won't be on little sticks like this." He grabs at the *piña* as though he never ate a pineapple before.

"Good, isn't it?" says one kid.

"*Deliciosa,*" says another.

"Paco . . ." I pull on his shirt, but he twists away

"It is delicious," says Nosey Nelson cheerfully. "We are enjoying the fruits of the Revolution! Before the Revolution, you poor kids didn't have enough to eat . . ."

I give up. Paco doesn't even notice me leaving. And as I walk home, I feel in such a daze I step into every crack and hole, and onto every board covering stinking puddles I always knew were there.

"How come Paco didn't want to hang out with me?" I ask Abuelo the minute I walk in the door.

"Don't worry," he says. "Paco is just hungry."

"But he had already eaten four *croquetas*—that was plenty of food," I say.

"Not just for food."

"What do you mean?" I ask.

"He might need other things."

"Like what?"

"His mother and father. Everybody needs their mother and father. Whether you are a revolutionary or not."

I pause. Did Abuelo mean *my* mother and father?

Ice Cream

Paco wants to go to the youth center, even when I invite him for ice cream.

"At the center, you get ice cream for free!" he giggles. "Especially when it's little kids' day, and guess what—it's little kids' day today!" he adds gleefully, rubbing his hands together like Count Dracula.

"But—"

"Never mind, just come!" he says. "Come on," he insists, pulling me along.

At the center, the kids run around like a hurricane.

"Let's get out of here, Paco," I whisper.

"Wait, just wait," Paco whispers back.

The lady with the *croquetas* last time winks at us and claps her hands, saying, "Come, everyone, let's sit in a nice circle." All the little kids do. "Now everybody close your eyes and pray for ice cream."

"What?" I say.

"Quiet," says Paco, shushing me. "Just watch! This is great!"

The little kids close their eyes, clasp their hands, and whisper, "Dear God, please give me ice cream."

"Now open your eyes!" says the lady suddenly. The kids open their eyes, but of course, there is no ice cream in front of them.

"Aww . . ." they moan in disappointment.

"What's going on, Paco?" I ask.

"Wait . . ." he says.

"You prayed for ice cream and didn't get it! Isn't that terrible?" teases the lady.

The little kids bleat "Yes," sounding like sheep. The lady goes on, "Now close your eyes and ask Fidel for ice cream."

"Hey, wait a minute," I whisper.

"Will you be quiet?!" says Paco, scolding me.

The kids close their eyes, whispering, "Dear Fidel, please give me ice cream." A big teenager comes out from the kitchen and puts an ice-cream pop in front of each kid!

"Now open your eyes," says the lady. The little kids' eyes widen when they see the ice-cream pops in front of them. They suck in their breath, surprised as lambs going to slaughter.

"See what Fidel did for you!" says the lady in fake amazement. "He gave you ice cream!"

The kids nod their heads meekly as they pick up their pops and lick. She winks at us before handing us pops as well. I refuse it! "Those kids were fooled," I say to Paco when I know she can't hear. "That was fake, Paco."

"So what, this ice cream is real," he says, taking a big lick.

"But those kids were tricked! They thought Fidel gave them ice cream," I say.

"So what?" says Paco, his eyes going wide. "They're just little kids."

"Would you like to be tricked?" I ask.

"I wouldn't mind if I got ice cream . . ." But suddenly he

is not looking at me—he is looking into the distance. For a minute, I think he has been taken over by space aliens or there was some poison in his ice cream because he drops his pop and runs. I follow with my eyes and see him jump into his parents' arms.

Reunion

They look different than the last time I saw them. His father looks like the American baseball player Willie Mays.

His mother is as pretty as an American movie star, even though she has a man's haircut.

"Son!" says his father, grabbing him and holding him up in the air.

"*Hijo*," screams his mother, covering him with kisses.

The ice-cream lady joins them, cheering almost. The little kids gather around the family, bleating—and then an image comes into my head. They look like a Black holy family: Mary and Joseph with Paco playing Baby Jesus and sheep bleating all around them in a manger—like in pictures in old calendars. It's stupid, but I can't shake it. They kiss and love Paco so much I think they all rise into the air.

The sight makes the ice cream sour in my stomach and come up all acidy in my throat. I turn to go, but slip and fall on Paco's dropped pop. Paco and his family turn to me from their high place to see what's happened and point and laugh. Paco, his parents, the bleating kids, the food lady, all of them laugh at me. I stand up and fly out of the room, my legs pumping, and don't stop until I get home to my *abuelo*, who is snoozing in front of the television.

"*¿Qué pasa?*" he says, alarmed to see me like this.

Words blurt out of my mouth. "Abuelo," I say, "why did they leave me! Tell me, Abuelo. Why did my parents leave me?"

Abuelo looks at me for a long moment. "What's the matter? What happened?"

"My parents, they left me. How could they have left me here and gone to the USA? Other parents stay. Other parents' love . . . love . . . love . . ." I can't finish my sentence because I am afraid of how it will end. Then it's as if I see my parent's wedding picture on the table for the first time. My mother's flowery hat looks cheerful, my father's dark suit serious. "Tell me!" I demand. "Why did they leave?"

Abuelo reaches for the wet cigar in his ashtray and fishes around for a match. His hand shakes a little as he tries to light it, so I grab the matches and light his cigar for him. He takes a few quick puffs, letting the smoke fill the room. When there is a cushion of smoke between us, he starts slowly.

"Your parents loved each other as children. Always playing together. Always sharing food. When they were six and eight years old, your father gave your mother his spinning top. When they were ten and twelve years old, she would mend his socks and oil his hair. He walked her everywhere she had to go to at night so she would be safe. He always carried the groceries when your grandmother sent her to the store."

"But what about me? What about me?"

"Let me finish! When your father got old enough, he shined shoes outside the clubs in Havana. The musicians loved him. Pretty soon the music snuck into his heart and soul and mind—your father got rumba fever so bad, beating congas day and night was all he wanted to do."

"I knew that! I knew he played the conga—"

"Let me finish," says Abuelo.

I wait.

"His hands were so fast they were like a flash!"

"Yes, I knew he was a good musician." I am getting impatient.

"Yes, but what you didn't know was that there was great interest in the north for mambo music. Your father wanted to go to New York to find his fortune playing conga there."

"But they both went? My mother *and* my father!"

"Not at first. At first, only your father went because it was such a great opportunity for him. The plan was for you and your mother to join him later. We were all so happy with the plan, even your *abuela*."

"So?"

"So he went, but your mother began to miss him so much, we decided she should go visit—just for a week—and come back. We borrowed money. She went. And then the accident happened."

He pauses. I wait.

"Your *abuela* never got over it. She got sick and died. And you want to know how come I didn't get sick and die? You want to know how I was able to go on and on?"

I wait.

"Because of you. Because I love you so much."

The orisha candle over the door flickers. The light lets me see what I really want to know. "Did my parents ever throw me up in the air and cover me with kisses and hugs all over?"

My grandfather looks me in the eye, seriously. "Every time they saw you," he says.

I lie back in my bed, tired.

But hours later, I wake up. The candles above my head have gone out.

I'm jealous of Paco.

Rebel Parents

"Paco," I call out to his window. He finally comes out on his balcony in his underwear. There are bits of fluff attached to his head.

"What?" he says sleepily.

"It's me," I say.

"What do you want?" he asks.

I pause because I don't know what I want.

"Come on up!" he says when I don't answer. "But be quiet. My parents are sleeping."

His apartment is completely different than before, clean and stink-free. The dishes are washed and put away. On the coffee table is a neat pile of posters of a young boy with a rifle in his hands.

"What's that?" I say.

"Can't you read, Mr. Genius?" snickers Paco. It says WILL HE BE A PATRIOT OR A TRAITOR? IT'S UP TO YOU. GIVE HIM REVOLUTIONARY INSTRUCTION.

"But what are you going to do with them?"

His parents come out of their bedroom. "*Hola*, Juan," says his mother. "Did you come to say good-bye?"

"I am not going anywhere," I say lamely.

"No, *we* are!" she laughs.

"All of us," adds Paco. "Together . . ."

"Yes, we're going all over the island . . ."

"To do what?" I ask.

"To put up posters, these posters. We want all kids to be patriots. The only way is for them to get revolutionary instruction!"

"But what about school?" I ask.

"Not a problem," say his mother.

"But—"

"We have to get going," she adds. "Would you like a poster?"

I have to say yes. They roll up a poster and stick it under my arm.

"We've got some packing to do," says his mother.

"Because this time I am going with them," adds Paco happily.

I give Paco a look that says, *Come outside*, but he doesn't get it.

"How long will you be gone?" I ask.

"I don't know," he answers. "However long it takes to do revolutionary work."

"Paco," says his mother. "Don't forget to pack extra underwear."

"I have to go," he grins at me.

And I turn away in case he runs to his mother and gets thrown up in the air to be covered with hugs and kisses.

The paper poster feels heavy under my arm as I walk home.

Macho

Time passes before I see Paco again. I am examining the juicer in my hand as I walk to Macho's garage for wire to fix it, remembering that day at the dump months ago, when Paco suddenly appears. He looks clean and neat, but there is something different about him too. Something I can't quite figure out. But then I do. He looks older.

"Paco," I say, excited to see him. "When did you get back?"

"Last night! It was wonderful. We went all over Cuba," he answers. "Putting revolutionary posters up everywhere. There are still so many people to revolutionize."

I want to bring him back to me. "Remember this juicer?" I ask. "We found it at the dump the day you hurt your knee."

He laughs. "You still have that old junk?"

"Well . . . yes. But I'm going to fix it. I'm just on my way to Macho's garage. Come with me."

We walk quietly, and for the first time ever, I search for something to say. "Remember when we became blood brothers?"

Paco shrugs. "Yes—kid stuff," he says. "Not really important."

We walk until all I hear are our steps. I jump at anything to say. "There's the *santeros*' house. Let's race and see who can get there first."

"No, I don't want to be seen around that house of *santería* . . . full of *orishas* and stuff . . ."

"What . . . why?"

Paco looks as though he is going to say something, but stops. "How about I race you to Macho's instead," and he takes off.

For a moment we are like the old days, blood brothers riding the wind and not thinking. Slowing down, I let him get to Macho's seconds before I do. We find Macho working under a convertible.

"Juan," says Macho from under the car. "I recognize those long legs!" He rolls out. "And you—how are you, Paco?"

"Bien," says Paco. "How come you don't have a poster up?"

"Huh?"

"A revolutionary poster. Like the one that says, '*Will he be a patriot or a traitor? It's up to you. Give him revolutionary instruction.*'"

"Oh well, I guess I never got one."

"I'll get you one!"

"You can have mine," I say.

"Okay," says Macho with some uncertainty. "What can I do for you?"

"I came to find a wire I need to fix this juicer," I say.

"Look around. Take anything you want."

I find the wire right away, then see a strip of rubber that gives me an idea. "Can I take this wire and this strip of rubber?" I ask.

"Sure, as long as you tell Mizcladia that I love her and can't live without her," Macho jokes.

"Got your little baby toys?" says Paco in a tone I don't like.

"What? No, wait—I'm going to make a road for Perfidia's toy car with this rubber and—" I stop. "Just come to my house and you'll see," I say. "I'll show you what I am going to do with these *toys*."

But as we enter our room, the candle for the *orisha* saints over our door fizzles out with a hiss. Paco looks up at our altar.

"My mother and father say you're not supposed to have any of those *orisha* altars anymore, you know. That's *santería* religion—you're not supposed to practice it anymore."

"But we've always had that over our door," I say weakly. "Ever since I ever knew you."

"Well, things have changed in Cuba, in case you haven't noticed." Then he smiles. "It's all right. My parents said we have to be patient with people like you."

I don't feel like showing him my projects anymore . . .

Then he says, "I've got to go to a committee meeting with my parents. Show me what you are going to do with your toys later."

Before I know it, he's gone. And I am glad.

Abuelo comes in from the kitchen. "Was that Paco?"

"Not really," I answer. "Not like he used to be."

I fix the juicer and take the strip of rubber to make a road for Perfidia's car. Macho comes over, and I make him and Mizcladia drinks with the juicer, but when I try to run the car on the strip of rubber as if it were a road, the car keeps falling over! My idea didn't work out like I thought. I throw the metal Matchbox toy against the wall; it makes a dent. Perfidia's face scrunches and she begins to cry.

Revolutionary Instruction

No marching today . . . worse. This time we are inside a classroom getting revolutionary instruction.

The instructor points to that poster that's everywhere and reads, "*'Will he be a patriot or a traitor? It's up to you. Give him revolutionary instruction.'* Revolutionary instruction is what we will have today! Now—what does *counter* mean?"

"It's a place you eat at," I whisper to Paco.

But he doesn't laugh. Instead he raises his hand and answers the question. "*Counter* means going against."

"Very good. So, what does *counterrevolution* mean?"

"It means going against the Revolution! Right?" Paco answers as if he was the smartest person in the room.

"Yes, who can give me an example?"

Again, Paco anwers quickly, "Trying to take valuable things with you when you leave Cuba is doing something that is counterrevolution. That's why people are only allowed to take two outfits when they leave."

Paco was never that quick in math class.

"That's right! Very good, Paco," says the instructor. "Anybody else?"

But Paco doesn't give anyone else the chance to answer. "I

know that sometimes even people who stay in Cuba hide their jewels," he says.

"Very good," says the instructor.

"Because they don't want the government to know how rich they are!"

My blood brother is a kiss-ass.

"Right again!" says the instructor, proud of Paco. "And it is our job to expose those dangerous people."

All at once I feel afraid—somehow stuck between the instructor and Paco.

"What would you do," the instructor goes on, "if your neighbor was hiding jewels?"

"I'd tell you," says Paco carefully.

"That means snitch on them," I whisper to Paco, putting fear aside.

"What would you do if your own parents were hiding jewels?"

"Tell you," says Paco.

"I wouldn't tell on my parents," I whisper to Paco.

Paco turns to me quickly. "You don't even have any parents," he says. "They got hit by a truck in Brooklyn, remember?"

I hit back with my own words. "What about you?" I say angrily. "What's the use of having parents if they leave you alone for so long?"

Paco's eyes go wide. "Yeah, well, they're not going away anymore. Not without me. Now they are home for good," he hisses.

"Class dismissed!" says the instructor.

I want to fight with Paco. "Would you snitch on me if I had lots of jewelry to hide?" I demand.

But then Paco's parents arrive to pick him up. He looks at me up and down, and sucks in his teeth. "Awww, man," he says. "You just don't get it, and you never will!"

And he runs to them.

Change

Arriba, abajo
Los yanquis son guanajos
Up, down, Americans are fools.

We march until a commotion breaks out nearby.

"Look!" cries Paco, pointing to a family of four. The young twin girls wear pretty white dresses. Their parents are dressed up too: the mother in heels and a big skirt, the father in a suit. They both carry suitcases. "Look—traitors," says Paco.

The family hears and picks up their step.

The *pioneros* turn to the family. Paco yells out, "Traitors! Look at them leaving Cuba for Miami! *¡Gusanos!*"

The family looks back, frightened, and runs a little faster.

"Let's get them!" screams Paco.

I grab him. "What are you doing? Stop!"

"Let go of me, they are traitors—can't you see?" he says, trying to shake himself loose.

"Leave them alone," I say. And I push him. Hard.

He falls to the ground and looks up at me, shocked and surprised, but jumps back at me like a spring! "Like I said yesterday," he hisses. "You just don't get it. You're in the same place you always were, and where you will always be!" Paco and the other *pioneros* keep chasing them, but I chase Paco. One twin falls. Her father picks her up, and they keep going. The other twin falls. This time, it's the mother who picks the kid up. They run.

Paco and I are running ahead of the pack like wolves, but since my legs are longer than his, I am able to lunge and grab him by the back of his *pionero* scarf and pull him down. That stops everybody. The family gets away as Paco glares at me.

Finally the instructor, all out of breath, catches up. "Let them go. We don't want people like them here in Cuba anyway!" Then he eyes us. "What's up with you two?"

We both say, "Nothing."

This is between us.

Paco the Spy

I push the fruit cart uphill, happy that there is no school today so I don't have to see Paco.

¡Frutas, naranjas dulces! sings Abuelo until he doubles over coughing so hard, we have to stop and sit on the Malecón wall.

"Are you okay, Abuelo?"

"*Sí, sí*, fine, not to worry," he says, catching his breath.

I sit with him until he looks over my shoulder and says, "Hey, there is your friend Paco."

My heart sinks. Sitting on the Malecón wall is Paco, near a lady and her baby carriage.

My grandfather waves him over. Paco takes a last look at the lady and her baby carriage and awkwardly joins us. We nod at each other. I busy myself with the fruit. Abuelo looks to each of us with glistening eyes, before filling in the silence. "Paco, what are you doing here?"

"Watching that woman," says Paco.

"That lady with the baby carriage?" asks Abuelo.

"Yes," he answers.

"Watching her do what?" I can't help asking.

"They look suspicious. That lady might be hiding something in that carriage."

His stupid statement makes me accidentally drop an orange

that rolls down the street. "What can they have in their baby carriage?" I ask, retrieving it.

"I don't know, but every time I go near them, they move away from me."

"Maybe because they think you are being creepy," I say.

Paco's eyes narrow as though he is taking aim.

But before anything can happen, an old customer, Don Reyes pulls up in his 1959 navy-blue Ford. He gets out and shuffles over. I think the curve in his back is even sharper than the last time I saw him at the rally so long ago when the bird crapped on Fidel's head. His straw fedora is pulled down to his ears. His shirt is soaked through with sweat. His eyes are pale blue and wet. Abuelo looks at him from under his own hat as they shake hands.

"How are you?" asks Abuelo.

"How can I be? Terrible," he grunts. "There's nothing on TV, I haven't been to the bathroom in two days, and my grandson, Miguel, has gone to the USA with his parents. Have you heard?"

"No," says Abuelo.

"I miss them."

"Why didn't you go with them?" asks Abuelo.

"Because I am not running away. Why should I leave my country because Fidel and his bunch of *comemierdas* crap eaters have taken over?"

"You should be careful what you say, *compadre*," says Paco.

Don Reyes looks at him. "How old are you, son?"

"Twelve," says Paco.

Don Reyes speaks into the wind, "We have sure come a long

strange way since that day at the rally when the dove crapped on Fidel's head."

"How about some juice?" says Abuelo quickly. "Juan made a juicer. Some juice will help you go to the bathroom."

"You know, you can never tell when there is a traitor among us," says Paco. "Even an old man with a fancy blue Ford, who can't go to the bathroom can be a traitor." Then he goes back to spy on the lady with the baby carriage.

Don Reyes looks after Paco, then whispers furtively, "If that's the youth of Cuba, I feel sorry for us all Adios." But he turns back quickly. "Oh—I'll take three naranjas, por favor. "No juice—if three oranges don't make me go—nothing will!"

He pays, and we watch him get into his car and almost hit a broken parking meter before driving away. Abuelo and I turn to each other. He is just about to say something when his eyes open wide and he bends over as if something had punched him in the stomach. Reaching for my arm, he gasps, "Juan take me home." Then he coughs and spits blood.

Escape

I get Abuelo home spitting and coughing all the way. But when we get there, we hear Mizcladia screaming from the back. "You cannot give up now," she yells. "We are so close to finishing."

Abuelo looks at me with eyes so watery I think he's crying. I help him into his chair. "Get me water, I'll be fine."

In the kitchen, I walk right into a fight between Mizcladia and Macho.

"Calm down, Mizcladia," Macho is saying in his rumbly deep voice. "I don't want to do it anymore. It was a crazy idea. We will drown, even if we don't get caught."

"I didn't think you were such a coward!" she screams, some of her pink hair rollers coming undone.

"Why can't we take a plane to New York City like everybody else?" says Macho.

"What are you, stupid?" she screeches. "We can't take a plane because we don't have the money! Only people with money can escape Cuba on a plane."

"That woman is a crazy person," Macho says the moment he sees me. "This love affair is over."

Suddenly a pink slipper whizzes by, just missing Macho's head. "*¡Me voy!*" he says, ducking out the door.

"*¡Cobarde!* Coward!" she yells after Macho.

"Whoa, *qué pasa*, calm down," I say.

"I can't calm down. How can I calm down? I am going to be stuck on this island forever, with these CDR so-called neighbors breathing down our necks all the time. And now Macho is gone! My chance to escape Cuba has just escaped! *¿Qué hago?*" Mizcladia screeches, rollers springing all around.

I had never thought of Cuba as a place to escape from.

"Come," she says to me. "I'll show you."

I follow her into the courtyard, and there is a rowboat with two inner tubes attached to either side.

"This boat was going to take us to Miami. But now Macho has chickened out! How will I get to Miami without a man!" says Mizcladia. By now her head looks like a mess of rollers and hair.

"You couldn't get anywhere in this boat even *with* a man," I say.

"What?"

"It has no rudder, no sail, no keel. No motor—nothing to make it go. There is no way this would work in the water!"

"What? What are those things?" she asks, surprised.

I go on to explain all the things I know about boats. Finally we just stand there, knee-deep in Mizcladia's disappointment.

"Look—I have to get Abuelo water," I say, going back into the kitchen as she follows. "His cough got really worse—"

But just then, I hear Abuelo coughing loudly, then fall with a thud.

Sick

Abuelo is on the floor, trying to catch his breath.

"I'll get some cough syrup," says Mizcladia.

"Abuelo!" I cry, trying to pick him up. "What's wrong?"

"Help me to my bed," he gasps. "I just stood up to see what was going on and—" He almost collapses in my arms.

Mizcladia comes back with the syrup. We try to give it to him, but he can hardly sit up. He bends over, coughing hard again. His eyes are bugged out. Tears run down the sides of his nose.

"Give him more *jarabe*!" I scream.

Mizcladia gives Abuelo more of the thick liquid. It makes him stop coughing, but just for a moment.

"Get Don Santo, the *santero*," says Mizcladia.

"*¿Por qué?*" I ask. "Why ask for Don Santo? Why a spiritualist? Is Abuelo going to die? Tell me! Tell me! Is he?"

"Just go!" she yells.

I run to Don Santo's house and knock on the door.

"*Entre*," he says in his high, old voice. He takes one look at me and says, "It's your *abuelo*—I know! I will get my things." He puts special beads around his neck, grabs grasses and incense from his cabinets, and follows me, moving quickly—like a bird flying, as if his long white shirt turned into wings. At the house,

- 264 -

the *santero* checks our altar. "Rum!" he calls out. I get him some rum and a glass. He pours a bit and offers it to Babalú Ayé, the orisha image over our door. Then he lights up a thick cigar, fills the space with smoke, waves his grasses around, and mutters.

Abuelo quiets down for a moment, but just as suddenly, Abuelo folds over coughing and spitting up even harder.

"Abuelo . . . !" I cry out.

"Go outside," says Mizcladia. "You are just in the way, really. We will take care of him."

I go outside and try to breathe, but it seems there is not enough air in the world.

Emergency

I look up, and my tears make the glittering stars soft and out of focus in the moonless sky. A shooting star shines bright, then fades and disappears into nothingness, and I think without my *abuelo* I will fade away too!

Tears come and go. I get hungry, eat a piece of fruit from the cart, then throw it up. The sight of the fruit makes me so sick I make sure I cover it under the tarp. Going into the house, I see nothing's changed. Inside, I hold back my tears; outside, I let them out. When I am calm, I return to Abuelo. He is better, but then suddenly he is worse.

This goes on all night. Finally, the sun shocks me by rising. How dare the sun rise and show its face like it's an ordinary day when Abuelo might be dying. I hear a car. It's Don Reyes's blue Ford. He parks right in front and gets out.

"Juan," he says nervously, looking in both directions, his watery blue eyes jumping all around. He is holding a bag the size of a loaf of bread.

"Juan, I need you to hide this for me. Just for a few days."

Before I can answer, Mizcladia calls out to me, "Juan!"

"Don Reyes," I say. "Abuelo is sick."

Don Reyes stares as if he doesn't understand what I am saying.

JUAN

"Juan!" Mizcladia calls out again.

"Abuelo is sick," I say again. "I have to go inside."

"I'll just hide this in the fruit cart!" says Don Reyes. "Right here! They are not checking fruit carts—not yet anyway," he adds, sticking the bag under the oranges.

Then—out of nowhere—Paco shows up! "What's going on?" he asks suspiciously.

"Have you been following me, you *estúpido* little kid?" says Don Reyes.

"I have to go," I say. Paco is the last person I want to see.

"I will help you," says Don Reyes, ignoring Paco and following me into the house.

Inside, Abuelo is a limp rag held up by Mizcladia—his head droops between his shoulders. The *santero* is chanting away. Don Reyes says, "We have to take him to the clinic. This is an emergency!"

We start out of the house. I run ahead to open the car door and help get Abuelo into the back seat.

"I'll stay here and keep an eye out," says Paco.

On what? I wonder. Then I know—Paco has been spying on Don Reyes since meeting him at the Malecón.

We drive off, and as I look out the window, I see Paco looking into the fruit cart.

Thanks

Abuelo coughs so suddenly I think his eyes will burst open.

"Hurry, Don Reyes, hurry," I beg.

I tremble. How many coughing eruptions can Abuelo take?

Taking him inside the clinic is like carrying a bag of air with bones in it. Paco's revolutionary posters are everywhere, screaming in my face, *Will he be a patriot or a traitor? It's up to you. Give him revolutionary instruction!*

There's a racket of crying kids, grown-ups moaning, the ding and dang sounds of metal tools hitting pans, a smell like Mercurochrome, and then a smell of old poop. Finally the fast, padded footsteps of a nurse in rubber-soled shoes.

"My goodness, this man looks terrible—come with me," she says, helping get him to a roomful of beds separated by curtains. "The doctor will be with you any moment," she instructs, showing us to a bed by a window.

"Thank you," I say.

She looks at Don Reyes. "You?"

"I am a friend," says Don Reyes.

"Good, he needs one," she snaps.

Abuelo sits on the bed. A young doctor with hair that flops over his forehead appears.

"We are here because of Abuelo's cough," I say. "He can hardly breathe."

"Of course. I can hear what a difficult time he is having. How long has he been coughing?" he asks, sliding the curtain shut for privacy and tossing his bangs back with a flick of his head.

I try to remember.

"Never mind," says the doctor, listening to Abuelo's chest. Finally he says, "I think this man has tuberculosis."

"Tuberculosis," I repeat like a dummy.

"I had never thought of that," says Don Reyes.

"Tuberculosis?" says Abuelo weakly. He had not thought of it either.

"Nurse!" the doctor calls out. "Give this man a sedative."

The nurse returns and gives Abuelo the medicine as the doctor turns to us. "Your *abuelo* must stay here a few days for tests. You might be infected too!"

"Me? But I feel fine," I say.

"You never know. But don't worry, we will take care of you both."

Abuelo looks at Don Reyes, tries to talk, but it's too much trouble.

"Don't worry about a thing," Don Reyes assures him. "I'll go back to your house and tell everybody where you are and take care of the fruit cart until you are both back."

"Thank you," I say.

"Of course."

Abuelo lets out a long string of farts.

"Thanks for letting me hide my bag," Don Reyes whispers so only I can hear. "I'll get it when the coast is clear," he adds.

I had forgotten all about Don Reyes's bag hidden in the fruit cart.

Secrets

"I am not sick," I tell Don Reyes when he finds us in the clinic days later. "But Abuelo must stay here a while longer." Abuelo nods, and we hear a string of flutter farts.

Don Reyes takes Abuelo's hand. "Don't worry about Juan," he says. "I will take care of him until you return."

Abuelo nods. He seems better. Don Reyes and I try to smile as we drive back to the house, but our smiles freeze the moment we get there.

Paco and a policeman are standing by the fruit cart. The policeman has Don Reyes's bag. Nosey Nelson is standing by, his eyes gleaming like a cat's. Don Reyes stops the car, cups his hand over his mouth, and whispers to me, "I will tell the policeman that you didn't know I put the bag in there."

We approach. Paco and I lock eyes.

"That's the man I saw hide the bag," says Paco, pointing at Don Reyes.

The policeman holds it up. Don Reyes almost falls back.

I feel so bad for Don Reyes, this poor, stooped-over old man who had helped me so much.

"What's in this?" asks the policeman.

Don Reyes stumbles where he stands.

"That's the man I saw hiding the bag," says Paco to the policeman. Then he sneers at Don Reyes, "How 'estúpido' do you think I am now, old man?" says Paco.

All at once, there is a rumble of fury in my ears. This is all Paco's fault. My anger travels from my gut to my fist, and almost as if it were not attached to me, my fist flies out from my body and lands in the middle of Paco's face! Paco falls backward.

"Hey, what's going on?" exclaims the policeman.

Paco charges me with all he's got, and then we scramble onto the ground, fists flying left and right, until the policeman takes out his billy club and hits the ground hard enough by our heads to make us stop.

"Get up! Both of you," he commands.

We get up, panting.

Suddenly Mizcladia comes out with two *cafecitos*.

"What's going on over here?" she says. Even as I taste the blood on my lips, I notice there is something different about her. And then I see—she is not wearing rollers and her hair is perfectly combed.

"I said, what's going on here?" Mizcladia repeats. "I come out here to give Nelson and this nice policeman a coffee and what do I find?" Mizcladia continues, "A common street fight!" She smiles and winks at both of them!

"Kid stuff," says the policeman, pushing us aside. "I'll come back for that coffee and whatever else later," he says, winking back. "Now I have to take Don Reyes in for questioning."

"What have I done?" says Don Reyes.

The policeman points to Paco. "This boy said you have tried to hide valuables. That is counterrevolutionary."

"Those are my personal possessions," says Don Reyes, grabbing at the bag and knocking it out of the policeman's hands. Everything spills out: an old Bible, a shiny necklace, pearl earrings, bracelets, a cameo, and a big wad of American money tied up with a rubber band.

Everyone freezes.

Revenge

"There's a lot of money there," says Mizcladia, eyes wide.

"Pick it up," says the policeman. I start to pick things up when the policeman stops me and says, "Not you! Him." He points to Don Reyes. "You!"

Don Reyes tries to get down, but his old knees betray him. He trips and falls on his face. I try to help him.

"Let him be," says the policeman. "I want *him* to pick it up."

Don Reyes picks up the Bible. "This was my mother's. Can I please . . . ?"

"Just gather it up," the policeman growls. "All of it."

Don Reyes picks up the cameo. "Please, this was my mother's . . ."

"All of it," says the policeman.

"Leave him alone," I say.

"Shut up, or I'll take you in too." Then he grabs the bag out of Don Reyes's hand, hustles him into the police car, and drives away.

I look at Mizcladia. And then at Paco.

"Get out! Go away!" I practically scream.

"What?" says Mizcladia.

"Not you! Him!" I say, pointing to Paco. "Paco, get away!"

Paco wipes at his bloody lip, gives me an angry look, and leaves.

JUAN

I am so angry I don't know what to do. I go inside to get away. How could Paco snitch on Don Reyes? I can't even think, blinking back the tears that keep trying to find a way out. What I want to do is hit! If Paco was going to be a snitch, I could be a snitch too. But how? On who? Walking around our room in circles, it finally comes to me.

Snitch

I rush to the courtyard. The stupid boat Mizcladia and Macho were going to escape in is still there. I will denounce Mizcladia. I will! I will tell everybody she was going to escape Cuba in a boat. It must be against the law somehow!

Just thinking of the way she smiled at the policeman and Nosey, even taking her hair rollers out for them, made me sick. And wanting to give them coffee! How could she! What a liar! What a fake!

I can just imagine the policeman's face when I tell him that Nosey Nelson was friends with Mizcladia, a woman who was getting a boat ready to escape Cuba with her boyfriend! Actually—getting friendly with a woman planning to escape Cuba makes Nosey Nelson guilty too, right?

I rush back to my front room and practically bump into Mizcladia quietly making more coffee in the kitchen. Her daughter, Perfidia, is on the floor playing with her little car on the strip of rubber and getting frustrated it doesn't stay on track!

Mizcladia and I look at each other sideways. I tell myself to be calm and cool down.

"Well," she says stupidly. "Don't worry. Don Reyes will be all right."

My coolness turns hot again and boils over quick. "How could you smile at that policeman like that?"

She turns to me in a flash. "Look, this is how it is in Cuba now. And you better learn to survive—quick! If I have to smile and give the policeman coffee so he might do some favors for me, then I will."

"But Don Reyes didn't deserve to be taken away just because he had a mother."

"What?"

"Because he wanted to keep some of his mother's things," I add.

"The Cuban people don't deserve Fidel either, but what can you do?" She shrugs. I can't believe what she is saying. Her words propel me out the door toward the police station to snitch on her.

Change of Heart

But just outside my house, I bump into Macho.

"Hey, Juan, just who I want to see," he says, grinning broadly.

"Huh? *¿Qué?*" I say stupidly.

He is carrying a covered dish. "Juan, how is your *abuelo*? I heard he was sick. Here is some soup. It's not much, but I thought you'd all like it."

Macho. I hadn't thought of him.

"I put plenty of cilantro in it!" says Macho. "It was good yesterday, which means it will be even better today." I look at his big, fat, friendly face. "There is a lot of garlic in it too, and you know my mother always said garlic was the best medicine in the whole world."

"Yes," I say, my anger slipping out, like air leaking out of a balloon.

"You take it in to him."

"He is not home. He is at the clinic . . ."

"Oh, well, anyway, you take it and eat it. I don't want to chance seeing Mizcladia. When she's mad, look out! She might throw a shoe at me."

"Yes, you are right," I say weakly.

"I love her and everything, but I have to wait for her to calm down."

"Yes," I say.

"And then I want to convince her to get rid of that boat. It could get her into big trouble if the authorities find out. It could get me into trouble for helping her!"

A sour feeling comes over me, and I start to feel sick. "Thanks, Macho," I say weakly, taking the bowl of soup. "Thanks."

"Hey, yes, you eat the soup."

"Thanks."

"And let me know if you need anything else," he says, giving me a big smile.

"Thanks." I go back into the house with the bowl of soup and sit on Abuelo's bed. Taking the foil off the soup fills our little space with the wonderful aromas of chicken, tomatoes, yuca, plantains, cilantro, and garlic. Without a spoon, I just bring it up to my lips and slurp. The soup warms my heart on its way to my stomach.

And I know one thing—whatever coming up Cuban makes me today in Cuba, it will not make me a snitch. I take a bigger swallow and I let it fill me up. It feels good.

Released

I won't be a snitch, but I will never go to school again. I will never be a *pionero,* and I will never be a friend to Paco either. As I wait for Abuelo to get well and come home, I go to the dump and decide to look only for things that are hard to come by since the Revolution. A typewriter, an electric fan, a can opener. These are things I can fix the way I could never fix things with Paco.

After selling the last of Abuelo's fruits and vegetables and throwing away what had rotted, I had covered up the pushcart and made money diving for coins. With *that* money, I bought milk and eggs.

It's only at night that I hate being alone in my room, so I go outside and look at the moon, which is all alone too. One night I see an old man shuffling up the street. It is Don Reyes. I run to him.

"Don Reyes," I say. "What happened?" He has a black eye and a cut on his head and has to twist his head and look at me from the side.

"My neck hurts from being in that cold cell," he says, "but I am okay. Fidel's crap eaters did not get the best of me."

I lead him into the house. "Come sit on Abuelo's bed," I say. He shows me his Bible and reaches into his pocket to pull out the cameo. "See—I still have my mother's Bible and cameo. And you want to know why?"

"Why?" I ask.

"Because before we got to the police station, I bribed the policeman with the American money. He took it. They are all crooks."

"I am sorry, Don Reyes," I say.

"No, it made me feel good."

"How come?" I ask, confused.

"Because it proves what I have always believed!" he says, with fire in his eyes. "That all of Fidel Castro's men are crap eaters—just like I always said. And now I can save this Bible and cameo for my grandson, Miguel."

"You know where they are?" I ask.

"Yes, Miguel is mowing lawns in Miami. He has a job! I know I'll see them again! He says there is a ground cover that grows in Miami that is similar to one that grows here. Maybe I'll visit when its flowers are in bloom."

He sighs, and then changes the subject. "What about your *abuelo*? How is he?"

I tell him about Abuelo's condition, and he promises he'll drive me to pick him up when the time comes.

Then I go into the kitchen. Mizcladia is making herself a snack, and Perfidia is on the floor, running her car along the strip of rubber I had forgotten all about. I make myself a drink as cold and icy as the feeling between Mizcladia and me. We say nothing. All we hear is Perfidia's car sliding along the rubber strip before it goes this way and that, and her frustrated grunts and groans that the car won't stay on the strip.

Then it comes to me! Of course, how stupid! The strip needs tracks!

I take a kitchen knife, and Perfidia watches as I carve out two tracks on the rubber strip. After a few tries, the car rolls on the tracks perfectly. Perfidia claps her fat little hands.

I breathe easily.

Abuelo Comes Home

Abuelo is home. He looks so much better but must still rest another couple of months. Abuelo listens closely as I tell him about Don Reyes's hidden bag in the fruit cart, and how I punched Paco in the face for snitching. "Don Reyes only wanted to keep the things that belonged to his mother," I say. "To remember her by. To someday send to his grandson, Miguel, in the USA." Then I add, "Miguel mows lawns there. Maybe I can fix or even design lawn mowers for him?"

Abuelo pulls me back. "Don Reyes has been a good friend to us," he says. Then he hesitates before saying, "And how is yours?"

"Huh? How is my what?" I ask, confused.

"Your good friend, Paco. How is he?"

"He is not my friend anymore! He is a snitch. I don't want to be his friend. I don't even want to go to school where I might see him, where I have to march around like a moron. I want to stay home and take care of you and dive for coins and sell fruit juice. That's it."

"And what about what I want?" he asks.

"What?"

"What about what *I* want?" he repeats.

"I don't know what you mean," I say.

"I want you to go back to school."

"But I don't want to! I don't want to be around those people. Those snitches!"

"You have to find a way to be in this new Cuba."

"That's what Mizcladia said!" I exclaim. "She couldn't have said something smart!"

"You have to find a way to rise past Fidel's shadow," he adds softly. "Listen to me—when I was in the clinic, they gave me some medicine that tasted like cow poop. They also stuck me with lots of needles. The bed was uncomfortable. I hated that stupid young doctor who kept telling me I should be grateful to Fidel for making medicine available for everybody . . . but the medicines and doctors *did* cure me!"

I listen. He goes on, "Sometimes you have to take bad stuff if it brings you some good."

"But what is good about being Paco's friend?" I demand to know.

"Maybe *nada*—nothing. You don't have to be his friend," says Abuelo. "You don't even have to be a *pionero*. You just have to go to school."

"But—"

"Just like I have to go back to that clinic when and if I can get my eyes fixed. They say I have cataracts and that they can take them away."

"But what about what they did to Don Reyes?" I insist. "And even what they did to Nelson. He was just a nice regular garbage collector, and now—I don't know—since he joined the Committees for the Defense of the Revolution he's become . . . I don't know . . . scary."

JUAN

Abuelo holds up his hand and gently places it on my arm. "We have to take what we can when we can get it." Before I can think about his words, he goes on, "You know what? Coming up Cuban has been hard for me too. I am old enough to know that things will change again in Cuba. Someday—I am sure of it. And I am happy that maybe, thanks to the new government, I will have healthy eyes to see those changes come. Maybe even to see Fidel being thrown out."

"But—"

"Get me some water, please," he says, putting his head back. In the kitchen, as Mizcladia fusses at the stove, Perfidia hands me her car. We play. The tiny car stays on the tracks just like it's supposed to.

Ex-Blood Brother

Arriba, abajo
Los yanquis son guanajos
Up, down, Americans are fools

I am sitting under a banyan tree working on a homework assignment. I have to draw gears and show how they could be used to propel a paddleboat. The *pioneros* are marching around without me. Paco is among them, yelling and screaming at them and telling them what to do.

They chant on and on until the instructor leading them says, "Let's take a short break." Then the *pionero* boys and girls spread out into little groups, each trying to find a bit of shade. I find the few remaining students who are not *pioneros*. There are fewer and fewer of us. Out of the corner of my eye I see Paco go into the school and come out with an ice-cream sandwich.

"Hey," he says, finally reaching me. "Want half?"

I shake my head and look away. Paco holds out his hand. I spit on the ground.

"Look," Paco says. "Denouncing Don Reyes was the right thing for me to do."

I still don't say anything.

"It's not only me that thinks so—my parents thought so too!"

"Really, your parents are still home?"

"Yes. You don't believe me, come over."

"No, I don't want to."

"Hey, you punched me in the face," he goes on. "Let's call it even, okay?"

When I don't say anything, he says, "I had to do it. A *pionero* has to do what a *pionero* has to do."

"Me too," I say.

"Huh?" Paco looks surprised.

"I have to do what I have to do, same as you."

"You just don't get it, do you?" he sneers.

"No," I answer, looking him in the eye. And I go back to my drawing. I don't look up until I hear Paco walking away. And in the time it takes him to disappear into the crowd of kids, I decide for sure to become an engineer, and think I could design some other kind of boat. I know I am going to figure this paddleboat gear problem out. I know I will keep looking for chances for a way out, if I stay on track. As I think about it, I try to find the little hole I had made in my finger to become Paco's blood brother. But of course, it's disappeared. Just like Paco.

The instructor calls the students back to marching and their stupid chant. Paco is the loudest at first, but then he just blends in with all the others.

Fidel, Fidel, qué tiene Fidel . . .

Que los americanos no pueden con él . . .

And I gather my things and I run as fast and free as the wind, enjoying the air and even the sweat that pours down my face and over my chest and down my long legs.

Free to be me . . .

Balseros

. . . and go to school. And every day after school, I go home and work on Mizcladia's boat in the courtyard. I'll keep working on it as long as I have to, until the gears are even stronger than my legs, so that someday maybe, if I want to, I'll be able to water-taxi the paddleboat all the way to America.

A Shared Heritage

HOW I CAME TO WRITE THIS BOOK

I always felt that Cuba, Puerto Rico, and the Dominican Republic were Caribbean sisters. Native Taino Indians freely canoed between the islands. When Europeans and Africans were thrown into the mix, Puerto Rico, Cuba, and Hispaniola came to share a similar Indigenous, Hispanic, and African culture.

But all three islands share a darker history. They were each bandied about by superpowers, suffering tumultuous internal historical events that eventually drove their people to the United States of America.

The twists and turns and dichotomy of Caribbean people have always interested me. Though I'm not Cuban, I was struck that if poverty drove my Puerto Rican family to the mainland in the 1940s, leaving middle-class Puerto Ricans behind, political unrest drove Cubans to the United States in 1959, leaving impoverished Cubans behind. While both—political unrest and poverty—drove Dominicans to the United States in the 1960s.

But what specifically made me want to write this particular book was this: I had decided to write a picture book about

Cuba. But as I did research to round out the story historically, my interest was piqued by the greater Cuban Revolution story in general.

First, I was stunned by the fact that over fourteen thousand unaccompanied Cuban minors were sent to the United States under a program, dubbed Operation Pedro Pan, by frightened parents who hoped to protect them from real or imagined Castro policies. And when I found out about the recruitment of young people called *brigadistas* to teach in Castro's literacy campaign, and then the revolutionary instruction that went on in schools under the *Pioneros* program, I was compelled to write about how these campaigns affected the lives of young people who stayed behind.

People's lives change by social and political movements whether they involve staying behind or venturing forth. I sometimes wonder what my life would have been like if my parents had stayed in Puerto Rico and I had been born there, instead of in New York and raised in the Bronx. I imagine Cubans wonder how their lives might have turned out if they had stayed in Cuba, or if Castro had never gained power.

I thought the young Cubans who emigrated to the United States, as well as those who stayed behind, were brave, valiant, funny, outrageous, loving, and resourceful. Reflecting on the displacements of my own people, I wondered what it would be like to be them. As I researched, I felt empathy for young people who managed to rise past Castro's shadow.

Finally, I couldn't help creating fictional characters

seen through the lens of my own Caribbean and human experience.

The result is the four stories I've crafted in *Coming Up Cuban*, painting one portrait punctuated by the experience, strength, and hope of Ana, Miguel, Zulema, and Juan.

—*Sonia Manzano*

More About Cuba

• I introduced Canadian tourists on page 20 after research showed me that Canada formally announced its recognition of the new Cuban government on January 8, 1959, the day the rebel army entered Havana. Though some Canadian officials expressed concern about the revolutionary tribunals taking place and acknowledged philosophical differences between the two countries, diplomatic relations between the Canada and Cuba remained uninterrupted in the aftermath of the Revolution.

• The *brigadistas* were young adults recruited by Fidel Castro to teach illiterate Cuban citizens to read. Many young people, bored with sedate lives, jumped at the chance to teach. For one year, they traveled the island bearing hammocks, notebooks, pencils, and kerosene lanterns to teach—but their goals were not completely altruistic. They promulgated Castro's political propaganda through the reading materials used.

The regime did eventually provide schools in rural areas, built by forced labor and prisoners..

• The *Pioneros* program was designed to teach revolutionary theory and instill revolutionary fervor to school-age children.

• José Martí (January 28, 1853–May 19, 1895) was a Cuban poet, philosopher, essayist, journalist, translator, professor, and publisher who is considered a Cuban national hero because of his role in the liberation of his country from the Spanish Empire in the nineteenth century.

His unification of the Cuban émigré community, particularly in Florida, was crucial to the success of the Cuban War of Independence against Spain. After his death, one of his poems from the book *Versos sencillos* (*Simple Verses*) was adapted to the song "Guantanamera," which has become the definitive patriotic song of Cuba. Following the 1959 Cuban Revolution, Martí's ideology became a major driving force in Cuban politics.

• Fidel Castro ruled Cuba until his death on November 25, 2016. His brother Raúl took over as his successor.

• I read about the Cuban peasant belief that night air, called *el sereno*, could make one sick, in my friend Luis Santeiro's memoir *Dancing with Dictators*. Though this could be a regional belief, I used it as an opportunity to mark the year 1961.

• Though there are differing perspectives among experts as to when the actual physical harassment of citizens began, I chose to insert that behavior earlier on, in Juan's life, to create dramatic impact.

• The word *gusanos*, applied to people leaving the country, is a term Fidel Castro used for the first time in a speech on January 2, 1961.

• There were several boat exodus movements from Cuba to Miami. The one I am suggesting Juan will grow up and join is the Mariel boat exodus that happened in 1980.

• A recently retrieved 1960 memo from Catholic Charities of Tottenville, Staten Island, helped me fill out Miguel's tale.

• Cultures can develop a collective memory. As I did my research, I read many references to a dove defecating on Castro's head that day at a rally. In some references, it was stated humorously; in others as a solemn sign of good luck; and in some books, it was attributed to a mechanical apparatus Castro had himself devised to make himself seem splendid! I found it in enough literature to believe it happened in one form or another.

• Finally, this book is based on real events, though I have compressed time in all the stories to build immediacy and drama. The editors, readers, and friends have done everything to help me make this book historically accurate. Any errors in authenticity are unintended, but strictly my own.

Timeline for Events Cited in This Book

1953

On July 26, Fidel attacked the Cuartel Moncada. That event gave name to Fidel's movement: Movimiento 26 de Julio.

1959

JANUARY

Fidel Castro enters Havana.

FEBRUARY

Many political prisoners are executed.

MAY

The first Agrarian Reform Law is signed in Cuba.

JULY

Fidel gives a speech in front of half a million Cuban peasants who came to Havana to celebrate the Agrarian Reform Law.

1960

SEPTEMBER

Castro creates neighborhood groups of citizens charged with keeping an eye out for counterrevolutionaries. They are called Committees for the Defense of the Revolution.

1961

JANUARY

The Cuban Literacy Campaign (Spanish: Campaña Nacional de Alfabetización en Cuba) was established. Counterrevolutionaries kill literacy campaign teacher Conrado Benítez.

FEBRUARY

Mount Loretto in Staten Island accepts Cuban refugee children.

APRIL

On April 17, 1961, USA backed Cuban and American paramilitaries, and landed on the Bay of Pigs beach in an attempt to take over the Cuban government. It overwhelmed a local revolutionary militia. However when the the international community found out about the invasion, U.S. President John F. Kennedy decided to withhold further support. The invading force was defeated within three days by the Cuban Revolutionary Armed Forces. Most of the invading counterrevolutionary troops were publicly interrogated and put into Cuban prisons.

The invasion was a US foreign policy failure, but it made Castro a national hero. Feeling he had proof the USA was trying to throw over his government, he militarized social initiatives. The US failure also widened the political division between the United States and Cuba, and pushed Cuba closer to the Soviet Union.

NOVEMBER

Counterrevolutionaries kill literacy campaign teacher Manuel Ascunce.

DECEMBER

Operation Pedro Pan begins.

THE FOLLOWING
Books and Resources
SERVED AS INSPIRATION FOR THIS NOVEL:

Books

Operation Pedro Pan by Yvonne M. Conde

Dancing with Dictators by Luis Santeiro

Learning to Die in Miami and *Waiting for Snow in Havana* by
Carlos Eire

The Red Umbrella by Christina Diaz Gonzalez

Fleeing Castro by Victor Andres Triay

90 Miles to Havana by Enrique Flores-Galbis

My Brigadista Year by Katherine Paterson

Refugee by Alan Gratz

The Cubans by Anthony DePalma

Documentaries

The Lost Apple, 2013, directed by Cliff Solway

We Will Meet Again, Season 2, Episode 5, "Escape from Cuba,"
PBS, 2019, hosted by Ann Curry

Maestra, 2012, directed by Catherine Murphy

Balseros, 2002, directed by Carles Bosch and Josep María
Domènech

Films

Before Night Falls, 2000, directed by Julian Schnabel. Based on the life of Cuban writer Reinaldo Arenas

Lucía, 1968, directed by Humberto Solás

Soy Cuba, 1964, directed by Mikhail Kalatozov

Memories of Underdevelopment, 1968, directed by Tomás Gutiérrez Alea

Acknowledgments

I want to thank my editor, Andrea Davis Pinkney, for not only encouraging me to go from picture book idea to novel idea, but for steering this book along its whole journey. *Gracias,* Andrea, for pointing out the most effective storylines in every draft you waded through.

Copy editor Jody Revenson and production editor Janell Harris deserve a round of applause for bringing out the best in every sentence.

Thank you creative director Elizabeth B. Parisi and illustrator Nicole Medina for evocative cover art—the first thing that grabs a reader's attention.

A special thanks goes to Eida del Risco, a professor at New York University, for her meticulous accuracy read on Cuban culture, historical facts, Spanish colloquialisms, and traditions during the height of Castro's rule, not to mention having special insight into Cuban humor. I am grateful for fellow writers Meg Medina's and Margarita Engle's comments. Their thoughts and opinions sharpened the tales.

Gracias, early draft readers, writers Luis Santeiro and Sally Cook, as well as scholars Maria de los Angeles Torres, professor of Latin American and Latino Studies at the University of Illinois in Chicago, who at six years old was one of the minors sent to the USA in the Pedro Pan program, and Lisandro Pérez, a professor of Latin American and Latinx Studies at John Jay College, City University of New York.

Thank you Enrique Flores-Galbis for chatting with me way back when this book was a tiny idea and telling me about Pedro Pan minors picking tomatoes.

Finally, take a bow, agent Jennifer Lyons, for supporting my every literary effort.

And it goes without saying, thanks to my husband, Richard Reagan, for reading every single word I write, and daughter, Gabriela Rose Reagan, for their support and for always reminding me of what's important.